CAUGHT UP!

Gwen Cannon

Caught Up

2012

Edited by: Patricia Barthwell

Cover Design: After the Ink.com

Published by Cannon Publishing 2012

ISBN 978-0-9676561-6-8

Printed in the United States of America

Acknowledgements

Hello family, friends, and new readers of my books;

I would like to thank God for giving me guidance, strength, and determination to create another spell binding novel. This book took me to a place I would never want to experience. But in fact, it is reality and it happens every day.

To my husband James (Jamo) who motivates and supports everything I do. Your genuine love and affection shows in everything you do. You gave insight and vision to my book and I thank you for that. Love you ba!

To my mother, the rock who has given me the knowledge and power that I can do all things, and never let anyone tear me down. You gave me strength and determination to knock down the road blocks in life.

To my boys, Corey, Jonathan, Jordan, Jalen, and Junior. Always remember;

take control of your life, don't let the people in your life take control of you.

To my sisters; Deborah I'm proud of the person you have become, God has truly blessed you; my sister Rosemary you are truly what the title of big sister is, you support, you listen, and you show that you truly care, you're a beautiful woman who believes in supporting your family no matter what the circumstances. My sister Rosilin, thanks so much for your support. My little sister, (lol) Margie Tabb who thinks she's my big sister, I appreciate and love you. We're more like friends then sisters. I would like to give a big thank you to someone I consider a big sister and long time family friend, Yvonne Burge, who supports me and so many ways. To my nieces; Kesha, my first and oldest niece, beautiful and strong, an avid reader, thanks for supporting me. My niece Catrea (Treetop) another avid reader of my books, thanks so much for your support. My nieces Reese, Brandi, Jessica, Kaela, Tosha, Jasmine, and Amauri. To my nephew, Lamar thanks for the support. Mrs. Nollie Etter, a fan for life who keeps me on my toes, asking "where is my book"? Lol, Mr. Kim, who truly let it be known that he believes in supporting. Your generosity is appreciated. To my hair stylist Kim Tyler, you keep it real and I appreciate and love the person you are. To my cousin Une, keep singing cuz, I'll see you at the top. To my friend/ co-worker, Toyia Baker, a beautiful person who keeps me focused at work, it's been so many days I wanted to just go the (F) off, Lol. To my friend Belinda Robinson, strong black woman who listens without judging, I know I'll definitely see you at the top! To my long, long, long time friend, Jackie Havard, we've been friends over forty years, thanks for supporting me sis. Oh, I can't forget Ms. Inge, thanks so much for the support. To the Crawford family, as my sister/friend Lettice Crawford once said; It takes a village to raise a child. You all are my village who supports and motivates me, that all things are possible. I thank you for your support! To my friends and devoted readers your continued support of my books will not go unnoticed. Words cannot express my appreciation of your support of my books.

I would like to send a special thank you to my nephew Antonio Collins, and friend Bufford they are in a place where they need strength, guidance and the love and support of their family. Thank you for your support of my books.

To my fellow local authors, Monique Mensah, author of Who is She To You, Inside Rain, and Smoke Screen, this young lady hit the literary world with explosives books that had me on the edge of my seat. Janaya Black; author of Beautiful Rage: The Break of Dawn, and the hit stage play The Breaking Point. Kennard Lajuan, author of Everything, But Not Enough, Monica Marie Jones, author of Floss, and Swag. Sylvia Hubbard author of so many books I've lost count, an awesome young lady who truly believes in supporting Michigan's local authors.

Caught Up

Prologue

Bam....I went tumbling backwards hitting my head on the glass cocktail table. I lay on the floor amongst the shattered pieces of broken glass, the blows to my chest were excruciating. It felt like someone had taken a slug hammer to my chest caving it in. As I struggled to get up, I could feel the glass cutting through my skin. I reached back to touch the back of my head, when I brought my hand up to my face, it was covered with blood. My vision became blurred, I felt faint, before I knew it, I passed out. I awoke dizzie, my vision was blurred, but someone was gently lowering my body into what felt like warm water. I could hear him sniffling, saying how sorry he was. “Baby, I promise I won’t do this again, please baby...say something” I refused to open my eyes, I just laid there in his arms with my eyes closed wishing God would help me escape from this monster.

Chapter 1

Mia

As I sit here, reminiscing over the events that took place today, I should have known he would come right in the house and knock the shit out me. I guess I had drunk a little too much of that bravery juice, 1800 silver will do it every-time. That shit will make you do things you wouldn't normally think of doing, like doing cart wheels in the living room. My day at work had been hectic, one of my

patients had committed suicide after finding out the injury he had sustained prevented him from continuing to play professional football. I just wanted to relax and take my mind off of the day's events. I should have opted for some wine, but I wanted something stronger, something I knew would take my mind off of the events that happened earlier that day and have me thinking about shit I shouldn't be thinking about. Isn't it funny how a little alcohol will have you doing and thinking about shit you wouldn't normally think about? The events that took place earlier that day is what set me off. I had called Troy's office checking to see if he wanted to do lunch or maybe dinner later. I just wanted to talk to my husband and spend a little quality time together, something that we both didn't' do much of lately. I instantly smiled when I heard Troy's secretary's voice. She had such a pleasant welcoming voice.
"Hi Mrs. Thomas, I'm sorry but Mr. Thomas is in a meeting with Taylor Tate"
"Don't bother Joyce, just tell him I called"
"I'll be sure to give him your message, have a nice day"

"You too Joyce" Click. After hearing Taylor's name I instantly got the ghetto girl, roll your eyes and neck attitude. I slammed my click board down and started rubbing along the back of my neck, I felt a headache coming on. I knew it was nothing but stress. I cancelled my appointments for the balance of the day and headed for the gym, I needed to work off some steam. Traffic was backed up on the lodge freeway, horns were honking and people were yelling out their car windows. My patience was starting to wear, my head was pounding now. The medicine I took before leaving the office wasn't taking affect. I pulled off on the next exit. The only thoughts going through my mind right now was Taylor Tate. I pulled over in the parking lot of MJ's Liquor store. I think I sat there for about thirty minutes before I finally went inside. My intention was to purchase a bottle of wine, but my mouth ordered Tiquila, 1800 Silver. I sat in the parking lot of the liquor store, took a couple of shots, closed my eyes and laid my head back against the headrest. The sultry sounds of Chrisette Michelle was vibrating throughout the car, "Epiphany"

"I'm leaving, I'm leaving…." So I think I'm just about over being your girlfriend….,I'm leaving, I'm leaving…..no more wondering what you've been doing, where you been sleeping….I'm leaving". Hmmm….just what I needed something to go straight to my head and a little music to sooth my nerves. After sitting in the parking lot for almost an hour I decided to call Troy's office again. This time I was directed to voice mail. With my bravery juice flowing inside of me I decided to leave a voice message. Not the usual "Baby I'm home, will you be working late?" Naw, I wanted this nigga to know exactly how I felt. You know the old saying, "Liquor makes you tell the truth". Well, my true feeling came out loud, and clear in that message. I don't know why the hell I decided on this day to be brave. I already knew what the outcome would be, once he came through that door.

****

The first few times Troy mentioned his new partner in the firm named Taylor, I assumed Taylor was a man the way Troy bragged. It was as if Taylor was God's gift to the firm, someone they had been long awaiting for to walk through the door and take the firm to another level. Troy would come home bragging, "Taylor did this, or Taylor handled that case". I couldn't wait to meet the almighty Taylor, who my husband came home every fucking day talking about Taylor did this, or Taylor handled a case and won. So, of course when I finally met Taylor face to face at the firm's annual Christmas party, I was blown away. Standing in front of me was this beautiful woman extending her perfectly manicured hand saying how she had heard so much about me and she was finally glad to meet me. I stood there dumb founded, and speechless, mumbling under my breath, *"so this is what my husband goes to work and see five days a week, eight to ten hours a day, this beautiful woman, who looks like a goddamn goddess?* Troy failed to mention that Taylor was a woman. She had on a pair of charcoal gray peep toe four inch Christian Louboutin's and she stood about 6ft with the heels on. She had long shapely legs, a tiny waist and an ass to die for. Her breasts probably sized at a 34 triple D. I could tell she had implants because she didn't have on a bra and they stood at attention waiting to be saluted. She walked with an air of confidence, like she owned the room. She exuded the attitude of, *"I don't give a fuck what anybody thinks about me"*. She had what a lot of women didn't possess, and that was high self-esteem, and the fact that she was holding her own. Taylor trickled confidence, and independence, with the steps she took; something I had lost when I started letting Troy tear me down. I admired Taylor in a weird, I hate your ass round- about way. I could tell she didn't half step when it came down to taking care of business. I guess that's why Troy would come home almost every fucking day saying something heroic that Taylor had assisted with in a case. My mind was reeling with what any woman in my position would be thinking; are they fucking? Because lately, he sure as hell wasn't fucking me!

****

So, here I am once again soaking in a tub of warm water, tapped off with some absons salt for opening my fucking mouth. The throbbing sensation seemed to be taking over my whole body. I rubbed along the inner part of my right thigh, tracing the blue and black bruise that had appeared, wishing the ache would go away. The pain in my chest was excruciating. I started rubbing my chest as if I could rub the pain away. I laid my head back against the edge of the porcelain Jacuzzi tub as the jets of water pulsated against my skin. I knew it would be another week before the blue and black bruises would fade back to my normal skin tone. I guess after years of being stomped, ravaged, and beat on, I had the healing process all the way down to the exact day. No one could have told me in a million years the man I married, who I stood before God, vowed to love, cherish and obey would turn out to be a monster. But in everyone's eyes, he was the perfect man. Little did anyone know, I was living in pure hell and was scared as fuck to leave. He told me If I ever tried to leave him, he would kill me first. To this day, I truly believe he would. You see, my husband is one of the highest paid attorney attorneys in Michigan. Yeah, my husband Troy had everyone fooled, even me before the beatings started.

Chapter 2

August 2001

Like so many women who think they've met Mr. Right, I met Troy Thomas in college. We were both freshmen attending Michigan State University in Lansing,

Michigan. Troy was born and raised on the south side of Chicago. He would strut around campus with his bad boy Chicago swag, jeans hanging just below his waist, timberland boots and a Polo shirt. Yeah, I have to admit, he was definitely eye candy, the kind of eye candy that made your yan, yan twitch. Me, I was born and raised in Southfield, Michigan. My mother was a single parent at the time, raising me on her own. I lost my father at the age of 14. He was shot and killed during a robbery at a gas station, located on Livernois, and Grand-River. From the reports, it stated that he was hit by random gunfire, but it wasn't long before it was determined that the bullet that took my father's life came from the robber. I remember the reporter on Channel 2 news, broadcasting my father's death. I sat in front of the T.V feeling numb inside. I attended every court hearing for my father's murder, I wanted to see with my own eyes that Justice would be served. It didn't take long for the jury to deliberate and come to a decision. The robber/murderer was given 25 to life. My mother sat in the court room holding my hand crying and praising God. After my father's passing, my mother was determined to make sure I continued to live the life style I had come accustomed to. She kept me in the latest fashion trends, and kept my hair tight. With my father gone, I didn't want to be a burden on my mother, so I helped out in any way I could. I knew she was trying to stay strong for me, but I would catch her crying and looking at old photos of her and my father. I knew that my parents had paid a lot of money for me to attend private school, and I was more than willing to attend public school to save money, but my mother wouldn't hear of it. She knew my father had put up a substantial amount of money in case of a rainy day. He called it, his emergency stash. Who calls putting over $200,000 away an emergency stash? My father's childhood was hard. His father was strung out on cocaine, and would make my father and his brother deliver drugs for the neighborhood drug dealer so that he could maintain his usual daily dose. He eventually died from a drug overdose. My father's mother was the backbone of the family. She worked two jobs, while trying to obtain her GED. His mother's motivation and drive is what made my father push me to reach higher than I possibly could, and not let anyone deter me from my dreams. With the insurance money from my father's death and the money he had put away, my mother paid up my tuition in full during high school, and paid my full tuition for Michigan State University. I started my freshmen year of college with a zero balance. Unlike my father, who paid his way through college working nights at a strip club, and writing term papers for students. He would charge $100.00 for a five page paper. Although my father was raised in the ghetto, he was smart as hell when it came to school. I remember my mother telling me how she loved the bad boy in him, and how attractive he was. She met my father during a visit to Michigan State. She remembered how he walked up to her, with a big smile on his face, extended his hand and introduced himself. She said all she could do was blush, but before she left, my father whispered in her ear that he was going to marry her. My mother never thought in a millions years that what my father whispered to her that day would come true. My mother said she saw a spark in him that she didn't' see in many men; a drive and passion to succeed. My mother would always tell him that she married the finest man in Michigan. After graduation, his drive and determination made him one of the top executives at Ford Motor Company. During his employment with Ford, he invested in several stock options. He knew which ones had the best turn around and those that wouldn't bring in a good profit. My father, God bless his soul, gave me and my mother the world. After his death, my mother started taking online classes to become a paralegal. She said it was something she always wanted to do, and it would keep her busy. In May of 2001, she graduated from Everest Institute. She was blessed to obtain a job at Smith and Trent law firm located in Southfield, Michigan. I could tell my mother was lonely, and missed my father. I saw a change in her after my father passed. She basically stayed to herself, and didn't socialize with any of her friends. She was so into making sure I had everything she failed to take time out for herself. I tried to convince her that I was okay, and to go out and have fun and enjoy herself. I was nineteen and about to attend my freshman year at Michigan State University. I was definitely looking forward to getting my party on. I had heard there was a party every weekend, and being at home, my mother wasn't trying to hear of her baby girl partying with anybody. At the start of my first semester, I would commute back and forth coming home every other weekend to check on my mom. But the commuting stopped once I laid eyes on Troy Thomas. I remember I used to call him Mr. Smooth. He had caramel smooth skin, pearly white teeth, a bald head, rock hard abs, and a tight ass to go with it. Yes, all the ladies in Case Hall Dorm knew of Troy Thomas. Walk into any dorm room, and the latest gossip was about who slept with who? And who wanted to get into Troy's pants? I didn't want to seem desperate, but damn....the nigga did make my poonany sing every time I saw him. I swear I could hear my pussy humming a love song. I felt guilty at first because at the time I was dating Chase Hunter. I met Chase my first day of school standing in line waiting to register for a math class that had just become available. I remember him tapping me on my shoulder asking if I had a pen. He had a Michigan State book bag thrown over his left shoulder. We started up a conversation standing in line, and a few weeks later we went on our first date. Now don't get me wrong, Chase was fine as hell too, he had hazel eyes and a bald head. Matter of fact Chase and Troy could easily pass for brothers. The only difference was they possessed very different life styles. Chase was more laid back, quiet, and basically stayed to him-self. Troy, on the other hand, was the center of attention wherever he went. He made his presence known when he walked into a room. He had what some ladies call swag. Everything about him was different, the way he dressed, and walked. He also had an air of confidence about himself.

****

"Hey beautiful" I looked up from my note book to see Troy Thomas standing in front of me with a killer smile. I almost wet my panties looking at him. I looked around me trying to figure out if this was a joke or what? Was somebody going to just out from behind a tree or something? But he just stood there smiling

"Heyyy......" I stuttered, feeling myself blushing like a little school girl.

"Hey!....is that all I get?" smiled Troy showing his pearly white teeth. I just sat there dumbfounded, lost for words, looking into his eyes. I didn't even know how to start off a normal conversation with this man. I started twirling my pen around between my fingers, while pulling my hair back behind my ear.

"Am I making you nervous?" Troy asked, while taking a seat directly across from me.

What the hell do this nigga want? I was thinking. I couldn't even look him straight in the eyes I was so damn nervous. He reached across the table and gently put his hand under my chin raising my head so that I was looking him directly in his hazel eyes, and my pussy started to sing again..... I guess I was smiling, because he asked me what was so funny. I told him I was thinking about something that happened earlier that day. (I lied) He got up and came around to my side of the table, bent down and whispered in my ear...."I know you're not shy, I've seen the way you walk into a room, stepping like you own it" He stood up and took a couple of steps backwards to watch my expression, then he sat back down. All I could do was smile and put my head down. Damn....this nigga been watching me for real? Yeah, he got me on that one, my mother always told me to walk with my head held high.

****

Reminiscing on those days, I did have confidence back then, but my husband has taken that away from me. He has totally destroyed the person I used to be. How can someone take back, what was taken away from them?

Chapter 3

Troy

"Taylor, are you free for lunch," asked Troy, while undressing her with his eyes.

"I have a meeting with a new client, and I wanted to look over the case before we meet, maybe we can get something to eat later" said Taylor, seductively licking her lips as she spoke. She knew how to turn

Troy on, and she used this to her advantage. She was hoping the firm would make her a partner, and she knew Troy could make it happen. She had only been with the firm six months. She started sleeping with Troy two weeks after she was hired. Taylor peeped Troy's hunger to get in her panties her first day of work. The receptionist was giving her a tour of the office and introducing her to the other attorneys located within the firm. Taylor put her Jessica Rabbit strut on while walking through the office. Heads were turning and even the women in the office were looking her up and down. She had an air about her that made you look twice. When she approached Troy, he practically tripped over his own feet he was so entranced with her beauty and pose. She was wearing a two-piece charcoal gray and red pinstriped skirt suit. It looked like it was tailor made for her body. The skirt was hugging her ass like a glove. The neckline of the jacket was cut deep, showing a peek of her breast as if she was teasing you with them. You could see the red lacy bra she was wearing with every movement she made. She had on a pair of 4 inch Red Micheal Kor's peep toe shoes. Her hair was pulled back in a bun, with little strands of hair falling in her face. She had an exotic look about her. Once Troy saw Taylor, he knew he had to have her, and he wasn't letting anyone or anything get in the way of getting into Taylor's bed, not even his wife.

Chapter 4

Mia

“Dr. Thomas, your 12 o’clock appointment is here,” said the receptionist standing in the doorway of Mia’s office. Mia looked nervously at the receptionist she wasn’t ready to face her next patient. It had been years since she had seen him, and she didn’t know if seeing him again would bring back old memories. Although she was married, she hadn’t forgotten her first love?

"Are you alright Dr. Thomas?" asked the receptionist looking at Mia with concern in her eyes.

"I'm okay Janice, thanks for asking, you can put Mr. Hunter in room three. I'll be with him shortly" said Mia still looking a little stressed.

"Okay Dr. Thomas" said the receptionist as she closed the door behind her. Mia started pacing back and forth across her office. She flopped down in her chair and pulled out a mirror and looked at herself closely. She started tracing the small dark circles that had started to appear around her eyes. She knew it was nothing but stress and not getting enough sleep. She pulled out her makeup compact and patted concealer around her eyes trying to masquerade the dark circles. She was glad her stylist talked her into cutting her hair. Her short curly locks made her look like Halle Berry. Her new hair-do had shaved ten years off her age. She gave herself another once over, got up straightened out her over coat and made her way down to room three. Mia kept opening, and closing her hands as she walked the long corridor to room three. She was wondering what he would say to her once she walked into the room. Would he remember her? Would he be glad to see her? Was he married? So many thoughts and questions were popping up in her head.

****

"Oh my God, it's can't be," he said, getting up off the examining table. Mia stood back while holding the chart against her chest smiling.
"It's me," she smiled. Before she could say another word, he lifted Mia off her feet, hugging and swinging her around at the same time. When he finally let go of Mia, he just stood there taking in all her beauty. In his eyes Mia hadn't changed a bit. Her short curly hair definitely made her look sexy as hell. Mia kept smiling. She couldn't believe Chase Hunter, her college sweetheart, was standing in front of her after ten long years. He still looked good as hell. He had a goatee that was trimmed ever so neatly lining his lips and down around his chin. There was something sexy, yet intoxicating about him. She couldn't put her finger on it.

"So what brings you here today Mr. Hunter?" breaking the silence in the room, while trying to stay professional. Yet, she couldn't help from blushing. She felt like she was back in college again.

"I tore a tendon in my knee playing basketball two days ago. The emergency room physician referred me to this clinic. Never in a million years did I think you would be the doctor walking through that door. Damn! Seeing you has made my day. Hey, I'm sorry Mi Mi, but I'm still tripping over seeing you. No way in hell did I get up this morning thinking I would see you. So how's life been treating you? Wait!...you don't have to answer that. Seeing... is believing. I always knew you would be successful. Look at you, a doctor. I'm so proud of you Mi Mi," smiled Chase

"It's Dr. Thomas," said Mia thinking back to how Chase always called her Mi Mi, instead of Mia. That was his nickname for her back then.

"I'm sorry...uhhhh Dr. Thomas" smiled Chase, while undressing Mia with his eyes. He kept looking her up and down as if she was a beautiful painting he was trying to memorize. She was feeling a little uncomfortable. She didn't know if it was Chase eye balling her, or just being in the same room with him after so many years. Mia started looking at his chart and the X-ray photos taken of his knee. "I need you to lie on your back, and scoot all the way to the top of the exam table. I want to check your knee. Your legs are so long, they're dangling off the end of the table," laughed Mia. "I'm going to add pressure to your knee, Let me know if it hurts when I put pressure on it"

"Right there, that's the spot," said Chase frowning up from the pressure being applied to his knee.

"Based on your injury and the X-rays, It looks like you have tendonitis. Some tendons in your knee were torn from the fall you took. You're lucky, I've seen worse cases. With a little therapy and some massage techniques, you should be back to normal in a few weeks. I want you to take it easy and don't do anything strenuous that involves your knee. In the meantime, I'm going to wrap a removable brace around your knee to keep it mobile. This will help the healing process. I prescribed some Motrin for pain, this will help the swelling also. The only time I want you to remove the brace is when you are bathing or going to bed for the night. Other than that, please keep it on, or you'll only do more damage."

"'Whatever you say Doc"

"Are you trying to be funny?" smiled Mia "No...of course not. You've always had a sense of humor, where did it go? You know I used to love to make you laugh" smiled Chase.

It had been a long time since Mia had anything to smile, or laugh about. Her life was a fucking nightmare. Her thoughts drifted back to Troy. The monster she had stood before God and vowed to love and obey. Why wasn't Troy more like Chase? Their only similarities were that they looked so much alike. Both were bald and the same height but they were totally different on their outlooks on life, and how they treated women.

****

"Mia, Mia, Dr. Thomas. Are you alright"?

"Yeah, I'm okay. Just a little tired, I didn't get much sleep last night"

"How's married life treating you?" asked Chase, trying to make conversation. He wasn't ready to go. He wanted to spend more time with Mia.
"Okay, I guess"

"You guess? What kind of answer is that? Your husband is a lucky man. I only wish I could have been that man." He said this with so much conviction that tears had welled up in Mia's eyes. She knew she had made the biggest mistake of her life when she left Chase for Troy. Chase was the better man, but Troy's suave and charming ways won her over. She knew she had broken Chase's heart and that was the reason he transferred to Wayne State University in Detroit, MI. She never heard from Chase after that. She even tried contacting him to see how he was doing, but he never returned any of her calls. Chase didn't know Mia kept a scrapbook of his accomplishments hidden away. She had read the various newspaper articles announcing where his artwork was being displayed. She even went to one of his openings, but by the time she arrived he had already left for Atlanta to do another art show. She attempted to tell him this, but thought it would be best left unsaid.

"Well Mr. Hunter, you are all set. Here's your prescription. You can put an ice pack on it twice a day that will help with the swelling also"

"Thanks Mia, I wish we had more time to catch up on things. Maybe if you have some free time next week, we can do lunch or maybe dinner for old time sake" Mia stood there not knowing how to respond to Chase. One part of her wanted to say "Hell yeah, I would love to go out to lunch with you" but the other part of her was saying, "Troy will swoop your ass if he found out you went out to lunch with Chase" Still, Mia was contemplating his offer.

"I'll tell you what, I have your number on file, and If I get some free time I'll call you and we can do lunch." Mia smiled just thinking about having lunch with Chase. It seemed like old memories of their relationship were starting to surface in her mind. To this day, she still beats herself up for leaving Chase. It wasn't like they were having problems in their relationship. Troy was just up in her face everyday, I guess you could say he was persistent. Chase sat there on the exam table watching Mia. There was something about her that didn't seem right. He couldn't put his finger on it, but he knew something wasn't right. They had dated for three years, and he always knew when something was bothering her. She would always take her right hand and rub her left arm up and down, as if she was trying to comfort herself, and Mia was standing in front of him now doing just that. She was holding his chart in her left hand against her chest and rubbing her left arm with her right hand going up and down her left arm.

"Mia, are you okay?"

"Yeah, I'm sorry. I drifted off there for a moment. Too much work and no play makes a girl stressed out" Mia said, trying to change the subject.

"Okay, so I'll be waiting on your call," smiled Chase.

Mia stopped Chase and asked, "Did you ever get married?" hoping he would say no. How could I be here thinking so selfishly of myself and I'm married.

"To answer your question, I was married to a beautiful caring woman. She died two years ago in a car accident, and no I'm not seeing anyone at the moment" said Chase, hoping his answer would sway Mia to go out to lunch with him.

"Wow....I'm so sorry Chase, I didn't know." Mia felt guilty for asking if he was married.

"It's okay; I'm taking one day at a time. They say prayer changes things, and I pray everyday, and I know God is helping me get through this. My day got brighter the moment I saw you walk through that door"

"Well, I'll give you a call for that lunch date" smiled Mia, as she was leaving the room. She stood outside the exam room with her back against the door holding his chart against her chest. She felt bad for Chase. She didn't know he had gotten married, and now to find out his wife died two years ago. Mia went back to her office and pulled out the scrapbook she had been keeping of Chase's accomplishments. She was looking over all the photos of him. He looked so happy and content. Chase's presence in the office left Mia smiling the rest of the day. The scent of his cologne was lingering, it brought a little happiness to her day. She wasn't looking forward to going home. A dark cloud seemed to form over her head at just that very thought.

Chapter 5

Jada

"Get your ass up nigga!" Jada screamed, smacking James on his naked ass. James lay sprawled across the bed on his stomach, with his face smothered in the pillow. He was trying to avoid getting into another argument with Jada, after last night's episode. She had cussed him out for letting a female walk up on him at the bar, and kiss him smack dead on the lips.

James rolled over, got up, stretched his arms upward, looked at Jada like she was crazy and made his way to the bathroom. The sound of water spurting from the showerhead could be heard as James started singing. He had a nice voice, so nice that he sang part-time on the weekends at Club Mystic in Farmington Hills. "Hey! how ya doing?" James was singing Jada's newest favorite tune by Jaheim, *"Ain't leaving without you"*. Jada was standing in front of the bedroom mirror humming the song right along with him, while pretending to ballroom. Jada had a beautiful voice too, but refused to let anyone but Mia hear her sing. She wanted to pursue her dream of becoming a fashion designer. She had an eye for fashion, and knew how to put a window display together where it would capture anyone's attention walking by. She worked for Macy's putting up displays for the women and men's apparel department.

James was still singing as he exited the shower "Don't know what your name is or who you came with, but I ain't leaving without you.....Hey girl how ya doing" He stood in front of the bathroom mirror drying off. Jada came up from behind and started kissing the nape of his neck. She knew James' sexual hot spot and knew this would make his soldier stand and salute. She started licking along the inner part of his back along his spine, making a wet streak from her tongue, while reaching around and grabbing his penis. She dropped to her knees, kissing and sucking on his ass, like it was a Georgia peach. As he turned around to face her, he tried to grab her up, but Jada was on a mission. She resisted his attempts to pull her up and instead put his penis in her mouth. She started sucking the tip like a lollipop. James almost lost his balance and leaned back against the sink. He closed his eyes and grabbed Jada's head while pushing his penis deeper into her mouth. He could feel the pressure of a volcanic eruption about to explode. The warmth and moisture of her mouth was so pleasurable he could no longer hold back. "Ahhhhhhhhh........damn baby...that shit felt so damn good" Still leaning against the sink with his eyes closed and knees shivering, James lifted himself up and headed back to the bedroom. He plopped down on the bed with his arms stretched out above his head. "You trying to kill a nigga?" He moaned.

Jada stood up and wiped her mouth with the back of her hand. "Hey!....how ya doing?" She sang as she danced around the bed laughing at James.

"Oh...you got jokes huh?"

"Aww...don't be like that. I was just taking care of my boo" Jada, licked her lips, satisfied that she had pleased her man. "I invited Mia to come see you sing tonight"

"That's straight. I got some new shit I've been working on. It's a duet, but I haven't found a good female vocalist to sing the part. We're lining up some auditions next week. If you know a female that can blow, let a brother know"

Jada stood watching James, as he got up from the bed, and proceeded to get dressed. In the back of her mind, she wanted to audition, but she didn't want James to make fun of her. God had blessed her with a beautiful voice, but she was shy when it came to letting anyone hear her sing. Mia was the only one who had ever heard Jada sing. She knew in her heart she would love to be on stage singing a duet with her man. The more she thought about it, she decided she would talk to Mia.

Chapter 6

Mia

"Jada, pickup. Damn it's going to voice mail. Hey Jada this is Mia. Troy won't be able to make it tonight. He has a late meeting with a client, but I'll be there to support James. See you later"
Beep.....Mia pushed the off button on the phone and set it down on the glass table in the living room. Before she could make it to the kitchen, her phone was blasting

Chrisette Michele's *"Blame it on me"* Mia pushed the talk button. "Hey Girlee, I just left you a voice message. Troy won't be coming with me tonight, but I will be sitting front and center to see James"

"You know I really don't care if your husband come or not. I didn't invite him anyway. Just as long as you're there," Jada's sarcasm didn't hide the fact she was glad Troy wasn't coming.

Mia knew Jada didn't care for Troy ever since she had found out he had been physically abusive. Jada tried on numerous occasions to convince Mia to leave him. But Mia wanted to make her marriage work. No matter how many times Troy had beaten her.
"Is there a cover charge?" asked Mia attempting to change the subject. She didn't want to get Jada started on Troy.

"Ten dollars at the door, but I got you, don't worry about it. Just ask for me when you get there"

"I'm glad you called me back, I wanted to talk to you about one of my patients today" Mia said smiling, thinking about her day at work.

"But I thought you weren't supposed to discuss your patients. Remember, patient

confidentiality," Jada questioned.
"Well, you actually know the patient that was in my office today"

"Who?" Jada asked wondering who Mia could possibly be talking about.

"Chase Hunter" His name slid off her lips with ease, as she smiled through the phone.

"Hell naw…Chase, Chase Hunter from MSU was in your office today? Does he still look good as hell? Is he single or married?"Jada was asking so many questions at one time, she didn't give Mia a chance to answer.

"Slow your ass down girl, laughed Mia. "No he's not married and yes he's single from what he's told me. The sad thing is that his wife died two years ago in a car accident"

"Damn…that's fucked up" Jada said, still waiting for Mia to tell her more. "Okay, what else did y'all talk about?" asked Jada, still being nosy.

"Nothing in particular, he did ask to take me out to lunch or dinner"

"I hope you said yes" said Jada

"I don't know if that's a good idea. I am married"

"Married but not dead, there's nothing wrong with going out to lunch with an old friend, although I know you shouldn't because you're married, but let's be real. Your husband is a hoe"

"Yeah...and that old friend of mine happens to be my ex-man, remember"

"Well, if it were me I would go out and enjoy myself for once. You deserve it Mia. I hate to say it, but your husband is an ass hole. He doesn't deserve you. He's probably fucking every female that works in his office" With that remark, Mia attempted to defend her husband.

"Jada, think what you want about Troy, but he's not that bad"

"Not that bad, not that bad! Wake up Mia. Catching your husband in bed with another woman is bad. Whatever the case, you know, and I know, Troy ain't SHIT! And you know I'm telling the truth. I think you are just holding on hoping and praying he'll change. It's not gonna happen Mia. You deserve better. I think there's a reason Chase showed up in your office. You might call it coincidence, but I call it a blessing in disguise. You should consider going out to lunch with him. What could it hurt? It's only food right?"

The more Jada talked, the more Mia was leaning toward taking Chase up on his lunch offer. Like Jada said, what could it hurt? It's only food.

Chapter 7

Troy

“Damn baby you really know how to please your man” Troy grabbed Taylor’s right breast and began massaging it. Taylor gave Troy a discerning look, from his comment.

“Ouch!...shit that hurt. Don’t be so fucking rough. Remember that’s my breast you're squeezing, not a fucking lemon" Taylor pulled away from Troy. She had been getting a little frustrated lately with his rough sex.

"Aw ..baby, you know I'm not trying to be rough. It's just that I get caught up in the moment and can't help myself" Troy, tried to ease the tension in the air.

"Well, I have to get back to the office. I have a client at 3 o'clock. I would hate to show up late and smelling like I just jumped off somebody's dick" Taylor said as she made her way to the bathroom to freshen up.

"Will I see you tonight?" hollered Troy from the bedroom

"You see me now Troy, I think we need to back up a little bit. Remember you have a wife at home. Or did you forget? She hadn't forgot his comment he made earlier about him being her man; "Please take note, that I am not exclusive to only you Troy. We're not a couple," said Taylor, as she reached down to pull her panties up.

Before she could say another word, Troy jumped up from the bed, stomped into the bathroom and grabbed her by the hair. He pulled so hard her neck looked like it was about to break in half. "Bitch! who the fuck do you think you're talking to?" Screamed Troy with fire in his eyes. He looked like a crazed maniac. This scene brought him back to when he was ten years old, and he witnessed his father break his mother's back. The only childhood memories that stood out for Troy was of his father beating his mother. Whenever he tried to intervene, his father would tell him that this was how you keep your woman in check. He could hear his father's words cutting so deep in his thoughts now. *"Boy, look at me....if a woman ever disrespects you. You snatch her ass up and let her know who's running the show. Always, always...remember that"* He said this with so much conviction that Troy thought beating a woman was the right thing to do. He thought it was what men should do. But, the beatings didn't start with Mia, they started when he was in high school.

Finally realizing what he was doing, Troy loosened his grip on Taylor's hair. He saw the fear in her eyes. When he looked up in the mirror, he didn't see himself. He saw the splitting image of his father. Taylor looked like a helpless little girl, begging for mercy. Before she could utter a word, Troy pulled her to his chest trying to comfort her. "Baby, I'm so sorry. I don't know what came over me. Please Taylor, you know I would never hurt you. It's just that I've been under so much stress lately. Please...Please forgive me." He grabbed her face and started kissing her tears as they flowed down her cheeks. You could see the fear in Taylor's eyes, as she pushed, and pulled to get away from Troy's grasp. The more she pulled, the harder he pulled her to him. His weight and strength overpowered her. She gave in, and let him caress the tears that wouldn't stop flowing.

Chapter 8

Mia

I don't know why I gave into having lunch with Chase. It just doesn't seem right. What if I bump into one of Troy's friends or co-workers? So many thoughts and questions were running through Mia's head including the (what if's) of the situation. But when Chase walked through the door, all the emotions and inclinations of what she should do disappeared. "Wow...you look...I'm speechless," said Mia, smiling from ear to ear. She felt like a schoolgirl on her first date. Chase looked like a hot caramel sundae draped with peanuts, ready to be eaten from head to toe. He had on a pair of Versace sun glasses, a two piece Michael Kors tan suit, with a white open collar shirt, and a pair of brown lace up Kenneth Cole shoes. He looked like he stepped straight out of the cover of GQ magazine.

"Aww...don't tease a brother. You are looking quite delicious yourself Mia," smiled Chase, undressing Mia with his eyes. Those damn hazel eyes, thought Mia. She was blushing from his compliment. She felt embarrassed that she couldn't remember the last time a man had even acknowledged the fact that she was beautiful. Even her own husband had slipped off the radar of giving her a compliment. She got up from her seat and gave Chase a friendly hug. Chase held on a little tighter. He didn't want to let go. He put his face to her hair and smelled the fresh scent of vanilla shampoo. He closed his eyes as if he wanted to stay in this relaxing place. Mia was trying to pull away, but at the same time it felt so right being in Chase's arms. He felt like her protector, like nothing could possibly go wrong, and then reality stepped in.

One of Mia's patients had come up to their table. "Hi Doctor Thomas, how are you? And this much be Mr. Thomas" Said Mia's patient extending his hand out to shake Chase's hand. "No Mr. Collins, this is an old college friend, Chase Hunter"

"Well hello Mr. Hunter, sorry I didn't mean to interrupt your lunch" Said the patient shaking Chase's hand and smiling looking at Mia like he had caught her in the act.

"Well it was nice seeing you Mr. Collins" Said Mia, hoping he would leave. Mr. Collins smiled at Mia, apologized for interrupting her lunch and turned and walked away, still looking back over his shoulder at her.

"Now that was weird" said Chase looking at Mia

"I know, sorry about that. Didn't think I would run into one of my patients"

"I think your patient Mr. Collins has a little crush on you. You didn't notice how he kept looking back at you like he wanted to slurp you up with some biscuits and syrup" Smiled Chase

"Whatever, he's old enough to be my father" Laughed Mia

"Hey, you can't blame the man. You are looking mighty delicious" Mia started blushing from Chase's remark.

"So how has life been treating you?" Asked Mia, while pulling her hand away from Chase. His eyes reminded her of Troy's. They both had beautiful hazel colored eyes that would have any woman mesmerized. Troy used his looks and those killer eyes to his advantage with women. Everywhere they would go some woman always gave him a compliment about how gorgeous his eyes were. Chase, on the other hand, was low-key, and nonchalant about the compliments he received. Mia started fidgeting with the buttons on her blouse. Without any indication, she instantly started rubbing her left arm with her right hand, going up and down. Chase noticed it right away; That nervous movement she does when something is bothering her. “Mia, is everything alright?” Chase asked with genuine concern in his eyes. He kept looking at Mia for some kind of indication that would tell him what was bothering her.

“I’m okay. I’ve been a little overworked at the office that’s all. I think I need a nice long overdue vacation. Maybe a nice getaway from everything,” Mia, tried not to show her true feelings. She knew that if she opened up to Chase, he would go after Troy, and she couldn’t bear for that to happen. She decided to keep her demons to herself and just enjoy her lunch date.

Chapter 9

When the abuse started

He was dating his high school sweetheart, Michelle Bradley. She was the senior editor of their high school paper, and Troy was the tight end on the football team. Just like Troy, Michelle was very popular amongst her peers. But Troy was extremely jealous of all the attention

Michelle received, especially during the times she had to interview someone on the football, basketball, or men's softball team. Even the fact that Michelle always let it be known to everyone that Troy Thomas was her man, it still didn't comfort Troy. He was always watching her every move. It was like he was infatuated with her, a type of stalker kind of love. One particular day, everyone decided to meet up at Bell Isle and put together an end of the summer party on the island. Everyone was looking forward to finding out what they had done over summer break. Michelle decided to drive her dad's car, because she didn't want to be stuck on the island too late. She knew her father would throw a fit if she came prancing in the house a minute late. As soon as she arrived, she went looking for Troy. One of his team-mates informed Michelle that Troy had gone walking along the bike trail. As Michelle walked along the path calling Troy's name every now and then, she came upon a bend in the road. She decided to go down one of the paths that looked like a short cut back onto the main road. As she was walking, she could hear moans coming from within the wooded path. Michelle's reporter instincts kicked in and she decided to make her way in the direction of the moans. She approached what looked like two individuals making out. At first, she got a thrill out of watching until she noticed the jersey thrown to the side. It looked exactly like the jersey Troy wore. He practically wore it everywhere they went. He called it his good luck charm. In the back of her mind, she was hoping and praying it was one of Troy's teammate's, but as she got closer, she made out the name and number on the jersey. She could hear the girl moaning his name. "Yes....ahhh....Troy, don't stop...right there...damn baby you feel so good" Michelle inched closer. She felt like she was in a trance looking at the movement of their bodies intertwined. The girl's legs were wrapped tightly around Troy's waist as he pounded himself into her woman hood. Michelle started to feel faint, everything seemed to be in slow motion. She could feel her mouth opening, but she couldn't hear any sound coming from it. She screamed as loud as she could; “Troy”! He jumped up off the girl, and started pulling and tugging on his jeans while almost tripping and falling. “Michelle, it’s not what you think, she came onto me” He stated as he pulled and tugged the jeans wrapped around his ankles. His female companion lazily got up smiling and licking her lips. She looked at Michelle, as if she was glad she had caught them in the act. Michelle turned to go back, as the tears swelled up in her eyes and started a long wet streak down her cheeks. Troy caught up with her, pulling at her trying to explain. Michelle snatched away from Troy’s grasp and smacked him across his face and spat at him. “I hate you Troy Thomas”

BAM! No one expected what happened next. Troy punched Michelle dead in her face. You could see the swelling almost instantly from the powerful impact of his punch. She went falling backwards to the hard graveled ground. She was out cold. Troy started shaking and pulling her. He started calling her name as if she would come to. At first, he thought she was dead, because her body was limp and made no movement, but he could see her chest rising up and down. She was breathing, but she was out. Troy picked her up and carried her back to the picnic area. Everyone was standing around drinking, and dancing. As he approached the crowd, his team-mate, Mike, ran up to him asking, “What happened man?”

“I don’t know, I was coming back through the wooded area, and came across Michelle lying passed out. I guess she must have tripped and bumped her head or something,” Troy, looked nervous as hell.

“It looks like hit the ground face forward. Look at her face man. It’s swollen and bruised” said Mike, pointing at the blue and black bruise forming on the right side of Michelle’s face.

“I better get her home” said Troy, wondering how the hell he was going to explain this to her parents. He knew her father was crazy as hell when it came to his baby girl. He was also afraid of what Michelle would do once she came to. In the back of his head, his only thought was going to jail. He didn’t want to destroy his only chance of receiving a full football scholarship. He decided to take Michelle to her car and wait for her to regain consciousness. He needed to explain to her what happened. Everyone was looking and trying to see what had happened to her. He grabbed a bottle of water and some paper towel from one of the picnic tables and proceeded to carry Michelle to her father's car. Once he approached the car he was glad to see that the door was unlocked. He would have had a hard time trying to hold Michelle, and get the keys out of her jean pocket. He gently sat her down in the passenger seat and reclined her seat back. He went around and climbed into the driver's seat, took the bottle of water, wet the paper towel and begin to dab ever so gently around the bruise that had formed on her face. Troy sat there for over thirty minutes dabbing her face and crying at the same time. He kept begging and pleading for God to forgive him. Snot was running down his face and he was blabbering like a little boy. He took the sleeve of his jersey and wiped his face. By now his eyes were blood shot red from crying.

****

"Where am I?" Said Michelle as she attempted to sit up. But her vision was blurred. She instantly reached to touch the swollen part of her face. It was painful to the touch. She looked at Troy like he was a stranger, someone she didn't know. As the tears formed in her eyes, the only thoughts running through her mind were why and how could Troy do this to her. She looked at him with unquestionable hatred.

"Michelle, please don't look at me like that. Let me explain. I don't know what made me hit you. Please...please you've got to believe me. I don't know what came over me. It was as if someone jumped inside my body and took control. I know I was wrong, but I'm begging you now. Please don't tell anyone I hit you. This will destroy me and my scholarship" Tears were running down his face. He mirrored a helpless little boy begging for mercy and forgiveness. Michelle knew she didn't hate him, as she looked over at him but, she genuinely felt sorry for him. She didn't know the extent of his childhood, or the many demons of his past. She was only aware that Troy never liked to discuss anything having to do with his family. Whenever she brought up the subject of his family, his whole demeanor changed. It was as if, a light switch was turned on, that he never wanted lit. After much pleading and begging, Michele decided not to let anyone know what really transpired that day on Belle Isle Island. She would go along with what Troy had told everyone, "*that she had tripped in the woods*". After that day, Michele never spoke to Troy again.

Chapter 10

Jada

"I want to know all the details, don't leave nothing out" Jada said, while stuffing her mouth with pizza.

"Damn....your ass is nosey. I don't kiss and tell," said Mia looking at Jada with a smile spread across her face. Jada was glad Mia decided to take Chase up on his offer to have lunch. She hadn't seen Mia this happy in a while. Mia and Chase genuinely enjoyed each other's company. They didn't want the lunch date to end. They decided to meet up for dinner in a week. It would have been sooner, but Chase had to go out of town for an art exhibit. Everything about their lunch date felt so right. Mia went home that night feeling a little less stressed.

******

"Earth to Mia, what are you over there day dreaming about. You had this big ass smile on your face. Damn...what did you and Mr. Hunter do besides eat?" Jada smiled, while stuffing the last slice of pizza in her mouth. "I want to know all the naughty dirty details and don't leave anything out"

"What makes you think anything naughty was going on? Laughed Mia, we only had lunch. We ate, we talked, and we got caught up on what we've been doing since graduating from college"

"Look at you, all happy and shit. That's the Mia I love to see. Girl you even look different. I know you got your hair cut and shit trying to do the sexy thing, but I can see it in your eyes" Jada was glad to see her friend smiling again. "I know you don't want to hear this, but you need to start looking out for yourself Mia. Start making Mia happy" Jada, reached over and gave her friend a hug. Mia grabbed Jada by the hand and started crying.

"What's wrong?" Jada asked with concern in her eyes. She was worried about Mia.

"Nothing, it's just that I've been thinking a lot over the past few days since I had lunch with Chase. I know I made the biggest mistake when I left him. Jada he is so kind and caring, and attentive. He's always been that way. He always knew when something was bothering me, and if I wasn't feeling well he would skip class to take care of me. I miss that Jada, someone who cares about me. Troy only thinks of himself, it's all about him. I don't know what to do. I've been living in misery the last few years trying to make my marriage work. I have to step back and ask myself, is it worth saving? Is Troy who I want to continue sharing my life with? A man who beats me for breakfast, lunch and dinner" Mia sat back in her chair, took out a piece of Kleenex and started dabbing around her eyes, trying not to smear her makeup.

"You're the only person who can answer that Mia. You already know how I feel about Troy. This is a decision you have to pray on, and ask God for guidance. He will move you to make the right decision. Just be careful. You know how any little thing can turn that crazy light switch on in Troy's head, and that you don't want to do. I pray for you Mia every night that God will watch over you, and that you will be okay. I know I never told you this, but when my phone rings late in the wee hours of the night, I dread answering it thinking that something terrible has happened to you. I love you Mia, you're the sister I never had. You know I will support any decision you make." Jada reached across the table and held Mia's hand. They both sat there staring at each other as if looking for any answer to Mia's problems.

Chapter 11

Taylor

Since the incident at the hotel, Troy and Taylor's hadn't spoken to each other in over a week. They kept it strictly professional. No business lunches or dinners. Any discussions or meetings regarding clients would be handled in the office. Taylor tried to keep as much distance between her and Troy as possible. Although she did miss their sexual rendezvous', she couldn't put the scene out of her head. Her only thought was how he was going to break her neck in half. Troy continuously tried to apologize. He sent several flower bouquets with notes attached stressing how sorry he was. She refused to put the flowers in her office she didn't want Troy to think she had forgiven him. In her mind, their relationship was over. There was no way in hell she was going to see him again. She had already been in one abusive relationship and she wasn't trying to get into another one. Besides, he was married. Troy's persistence was starting to get the best of Taylor. She knew they had to work together, and she was trying desperately to keep it professional. At one time, she even threatened Troy with telling his wife about them if he didn't leave her alone but it didn't seem to faze him at all. Apparently, he was fixated on getting Taylor back.

Chapter 12

Mia

"What should I wear tonight? It's been so long since I've been out on a real date. Lately, the only time I go out is with Jada at one of James' gigs, or one of Troy's office functions. I doubt if Troy even notices I'm gone. Lately, he's been working late at the office and usually doesn't get home until around 10:00pm. I should be home, and in bed by the time he hits the door". Mia was in the mirror trying to decide if she should wear the black strapless dress, or the royal blue BCBG dress with one shoulder exposed. Both dresses made her look sexy as hell. She decided on the royal blue, since the weather outside was sunny. As she was slipping the dress over her head, she could hear the sound of keys in the door. I know damn well Troy isn't home this early in the day, she thought. Before Mia could pull the dress off, Troy came strolling in the bedroom.

"Damn! Where you about to go, all dressed up?" Troy looked Mia up and down, examining her outfit. The dress was hugging her ass like a glove and it showed off all her curves. She didn't have on any undergarments and the in-print of her nipples were showing through the dress. He stood back with his arms folded across his chest looking at her. He couldn't remember the last time he had sex with his wife. He wasn't really keeping count, seeing that he was in Taylor's bed almost every other day. But, in the last few weeks, Taylor was not trying to have anything to do with Troy. He didn't' know if it was the absence of not having sex in weeks, or his wife was looking sexy as hell in that dress. Troy walked over to Mia and reached out his hand. At first, Mia raised her arms in defense. After all, she was ready to block whatever punches he was about to throw her way. But, instead of hitting her, his hand went to her right breast. Mia didn't know how to react. She just stood with her arms at her side watching Troy as he started to massage her breast. It had been a while since she had any sexual encounter with her husband, or anyone else. She didn't even know if Troy still found her sexually attractive. To keep peace, she kept her thoughts to herself about their non-existent sex life. Troy kept massaging her breast until her nipple was rock hard. He put his mouth to the in-print of her nipple on the dress and started sucking on it, forming a wet spot He began flicking his tongue across her nipple and didn't seem to care that he was ruining her dress. Mia didn't dare move, she didn't' want to cause any crazed reaction from Troy, but the sensation from his sucking was building up a heat wave between her legs. She could feel the moisture forming. Her pussy was screaming to be stroked. Mia grabbed at his belt buckle, clumsily trying to unbuckle his pants. Troy pushed her hand away, undid his pants, and let them drop to his ankles. As he stepped out of his pants, he lifted Mia up as she wrapped her legs around him. Troy didn't realize she didn't have on any panties until he grabbed her ass. This seemed to make him even more aroused. He looked in Mia's eyes with a sexual desire she hadn't seen in years. He holstered her up in the air, as his penis slid into the volcanic hole that was dripping with hot lava. Their bodies started moving in unison. Mia reached up and grabbed a hold of his bald head, holding on for dear life. She was going up and down on his penis like she was galloping on a horse. She could feel her pussy contracting and squeezing his dick. She knew what she was doing, because Troy started pounding his penis into her, while trying to suck her breast. He was sucking so hard, that Mia was moaning with pain, but he thought her moans were of sexual desire. Mia held onto Troy pounding away on his dick. The harder she pounded, she felt her volcanic hole erupting with hot juices she hadn't felt in weeks. Her screams of pleasure could be heard throughout their 4000 square foot condo. Troy closed his eyes trying to maintain his balance. He held Mia, while still pounding his dick into her. He felt the explosion he so needed to release. "Aahhhhh.........." their wet sex juices slowly started a wet stream down his inner thigh. He put his face into Mia's chest, trying to catch his breath. His legs felt like a ton of bricks were laying on them. He stumbled almost tripping while carrying Mia over to the bed. He plopped down next to her, and started snoring immediately. Mia lay with her eyes closed, drifting off to sleep into another world where everything was perfect, even her marriage. She had completely forgotten about her date with Chase.

****

Chase sat at the restaurant. He looked out into the street waiting patiently for Mia to arrive. He kept looking down at his watch, checking the time. He had a worried look on his face. It had been well over thirty minutes since he had last talked to her. He didn't know if he should call, or wait a little longer. He decided to call. The beeping of Mia's phone brought Troy out of a deep sleep. He looked over at Mia, who was snoring lightly. He got up, went over to the dresser and looked down at her phone. The veins on the side of his head started forming as he looked at the name flashing across the screen. "*Chase Hunter*"

Chapter 13

Jada

Jada kept prancing back and forth from the living room to the kitchen. She couldn't keep still she was so upset. "If you don't go to the police, I damn sure will. You can barely fucking walk. Look at you Mia," screamed Jada, with tears forming in her eyes. "What the fuck did that crazy motherfucka hit you with?" Mia was crunched up in a ball on the couch visibly in pain. She was holding her robe tightly around her waist as if it was a security blanket. She looked like she had been in a war zone. Her hair was matted to her head, and her eyes were swollen from crying. Jada made her open her robe, because she knew from previous beatings that Troy never hit Mia in her face. His punishment was always to her body. Looking at her from the outside no one would ever know the beatings she experienced at the hands of Troy. Jada knew instantly something was wrong when she hadn't heard from Mia in two days. She had tried calling her cell phone and kept getting sent to her voice mail. After calling her office, the receptionist had told her that Mia was out sick, and hadn't been in the office in a couple of days. Jada knew something wasn't right. No matter what, they always made sure to check in with each other every day. Even if it was just to say *"I love you sista girl!"* That's when Jada decided to drive by without even giving Mia notice. She knew if she left her a message saying she was going to stop by, Mia probably would have left. She never thought that she would walk in and find her friend in the state that she was in. After an hour of crying and holding each other, Jada finally convinced Mia to go to the hospital.

****

"After looking at your X-rays, and based on the symptoms you described, the pain in your chest, difficulty breathing, and pain from movement, you fractured your rib cage Dr. Thomas. Do you want to tell me how this happened?" the doctor said while frowning up his brow and looking down over his glasses.
"I slipped and fell in the shower" Mia said in pain, while the doctor applied pressure to her rib cage.

"Hmmm...okay if that's what you say happened Dr. Thomas. I'll put that on your chart, but based on your x-rays, you have other internal bruising that showed up on your images. Is there something you want to tell me?" He knew the signs of abuse; he had seen it so many times in his twenty-two years of experience. He was worried that a more tragic ending would eventually happen if this wasn't taken care of.

"Trust me Dr. King, I'm okay. Just wrap my ribs, and give me some Motrin, that's all I need. I tried to tell my sister I was okay, but she insisted I come into the clinic"

"I'm glad you listened to your sister. You should be glad you have a sister who cares about your well being"

Mia was staring off into space, looking at a picture on the wall of children running around at a carnival with big balloons. It brought her back to her childhood days, when everything was nice and pleasant. No pain, no worries, just playing with her friends. She was thinking of why her marriage wasn't like her parents. They always seemed so happy, although they had their disagreements she never saw her father raise his hand to her mother. He always showed her love. She could remember her father's words; *"a man should never put his hands on a woman, he should walk away first". Mia* thought about her marriage to Troy. Did he truly love her? And if he did, why would he continue to hurt her? Tears welled up in Mia's eyes. Dr. King walked over to Mia and handed her a Kleenex. He stood with her chart in his hands, and said, "If you need to talk to someone, I can refer you to Dr. Odom, she specializes in family crisis, amongst other things". He pulled out a pad, scribbled Dr. Odom's information down, and handed the paper to Mia. As a professional in the medical field, Mia felt a little embarrassed. She held her head down as she reached for the paper. The doctor must have felt this from Mia, when he said, "There's nothing to be ashamed of Dr. Thomas, we're all humans, and we all make mistakes. I don't want you leaving here feeling like you've done something wrong. Here's your prescription, and please consider making an appointment with Dr. Odom, I guarantee you won't regret it" As he handed the prescription to her, he smiled hoping it would cheer her up.

"Thanks Dr. King" Mia smiled, trying to hide her true emotions.

Mia knew everything the doctor was telling her was true. She did need help, and deep down inside she knew the beatings were not going to stop, no matter how much counseling or talking to Troy. She knew because they had tried counseling years ago. At first, she thought the sessions were working because Troy had stopped beating on her. He was actually treating her like any normal husband would treat his wife, someone who stood before God and promised to take care of. But after three beautiful months of happiness, the beating started up again with the first disagreement they had. It was like whatever he said was written in stone. Troy didn't value her opinion, or her. She knew what had to be done, but would she have the strength and courage to make it happen. Only time would tell.

Chapter 14

Chase

Chase was trying to busy himself with painting. He had been worried about Mia. It was going on two weeks, and she hadn't returned any of his phone calls. He just wanted to make sure she was okay because she never showed up for their dinner date. He had waited at the restaurant over two hours. When he tried calling her cell phone it went straight to voice mail. He had left several voice messages pleading for her to call him back and let him know she was alright. He was hoping she hadn't gotten into an accident or something worse. Today, He was wondering if he should just drop by her office, but he didn't' want to seem overbearing. They were just rekindling their friendship, and he didn't want Mia to push him away. After all these years, he still cared deeply for her. She was his first true love, someone who could relate to him not only in a physical way, but mentally and emotionally. It was as if he had met his soul mate. After their lunch date, all the feelings that he had tried so desperately to bury, had re-surfaced. He knew deep down inside, his love for Mia had never faded away but was locked away buried deep in his heart. Although she had left him for Troy, he never stopped loving her. He felt their encounter wasn't a coincidence, but was faith. He had been hoping and praying that one day he would bump into her in the street and confess his love to her. The initial shock was that he had no idea she had actually married Troy Thomas. Chase knew Troy was a womanizer in college, and felt that he would never change. That's why it hurt him so much when Mia broke it off with him to be with Troy. Now after all these years, as luck would have it, Mia had surfaced back into his life. And he wasn't letting anyone or anything get in the way of having her back. Not even her husband Troy.

Chapter 15

Jada

Jada hadn't told James that she was auditioning for the duet his band had posted. She wanted to surprise him. She was glad Mia had talked her into it. She had decided to use the name Tina when she went into the studio to register for the audition. Mia worked a half day to be with Jada as her support system. Mia was more excited about the audition than

Jada. She was glad to see her friend finally using the special gift she was blessed with. Jada made sure to let Mia know that James had no clue that she was auditioning. When they arrived at the lounge, there were about thirty females waiting in line at the door to get in. A tall muscular gentleman was posted at the entrance with a clip board in hand, checking off the names as they arrived, and requesting a picture ID. Jada instantly got nervous. She had no idea they would be checking ID's against the list of names. She knew she had registered with a fictious name.
"Jada, what's wrong?" asked Mia, She could see that Jada was nervous.
"Girl, I didn't' know they would be checking for ID"

"What's wrong with that? I know you got ID" said Mia, looking at Jada sideways wondering what was going on.

"Yeah, I have ID that says Jada Jones, not Tina Jones"

"What the hell...you signed up for the audition with the wrong name? Why did you do that?" asked Mia, looking at her like she was crazy.

"It's not what you think. I told you I didn't want James to know I was auditioning. I wanted to surprise him"

"Well you got a surprise alright. Now you have to think of something to get your ass in there. I didn't work a half day for nothing. I'm going to hear my friend sing today, or my name ain't Mia Thomas" They both started laughing.

"Ok, we got to think of something and quick" said Jada, bouncing side to side. "Leave it to me. I have an idea" Mia responded. Whatever Mia was saying to the man at the door, it worked. After about five minutes of talking, Mia was handing the man her business card and waving for Jada to come on.
"What the hell did you say to him" Jada, looked at Mia frowning up her eye brow

"I saw the way he kept rubbing the back of his neck like he was trying to rub out a cramp or something. I just offered my services as a Physical Therapist. Told him I would throw in a free-bee and help him with his neck if he let my sister in right now. He said his neck has been bothering him for almost a month. He jumped at the offer"

By the way, your fake ass name was at the bottom of the list and I sure as hell wasn't waiting for twenty-nine other chicks to sing.
"I just love you..." smiled Jada, hugging Mia
"Now get your ass in there and blow the house down" Mia laughed as she pushed Jada through the door.

****

James first initial reaction when Jada came onto the stage was; "*What the fuck is she doing here? I must be getting punked or something*" is what James told one of the band members! But when Jada put the mike up to her mouth and started belting out the song, James was speechless. He just sat there in awe. He was totally blown away with the sound of Jada's voice. It was so smooth, medolic, and soulful. He couldn't believe the woman he had been dating for over three years, and had grown to love was hiding such a treasure. When Jada finished the verse she was instructed to sing, the room was silent.
"Baby, baby, say something" said Jada, looking at James for confirmation.
"What the hell" James hollered. Jada looked at James shocked at his response. She didn't know how to react. *"Damn,*

was I that bad?" Jada wondered but before she could respond to James outburst, he said; "Baby you can sing your ass off and I ain't saying that just because you're my woman. You can sing baby!" Mia was sitting down in the back of the lounge with tears rolling down her cheeks. She was so proud of her friend. She stood up and started clapping. Before you knew it, everyone in the lounge was standing up, giving Jada a standing ovation. Jada stood on the stage smiling and taking a bow. She wished she could have wrapped that very moment up and took it home with her. It felt so right being there on the stage with everyone standing, and clapping. At that moment, she knew this was what she was born to do. After the audition, they met up with James at Chili's. When James arrived, he walked right up to Jada and started tonguing her down right in front of everybody.
"Damn...get a room," laughed Mia leaning back in her chair.
"Down tiger" smiled Jada, while licking her lips.

"Ladies, I hate to cut this little celebration short, but I need my baby to come with me right now" said James, extending his hand out to Jada.
"Alrighty then, you don't have to tell me

twice. I'll see y'all later, call me tomorrow Jada" Mia got up from the table and took one last swallow from her apple martini. "No Mia, I need you to come with us too", James instructed.
"Baby, what's going on" said Jada, smiling at James wondering what the hell was he up to?. They got in Mia's car, and followed James. They pulled up to a club called Epiphany in Royal Oak. The outside of the club was lit up with various shades of blue lighting. "Come on ladies, we go on stage in ten minutes" said James walking up to Jada and Mia.

"Wait, wait....what did you say?" Jada stuttered nervously as she pulled James by the arm. She looked at him as if he had spoken a foreign language.

"I said, we go on stage in ten minutes. Now come on baby, we got to warm up a little". Mia looked from Jada to James, wondering who was going to speak first. "Okay James, you're joking right?" Jada asked, looking nervous as hell.

"No, I'm not. I made a call to my boy Rick, he's the owner of Epiphany. I asked him if he could pull some strings and let me and my baby do one song" James, smiled at Jada. He was so excited after he heard Jada sing, he couldn't wait to get her on

stage.
"Baby, I'm not ready to sing anything right now" Jada exclaimed, while shaking her head no.
"Come on baby, just one song. Pleaseeeeee" begged James, as he grabbed Jada and pulled her to him. James embraced Jada and was whispering in her ear.
A big smile appeared on her face.
"Damn...what was he whispering in your ear?" asked Mia smiling.
"All I can say is that I won't be going to work in the morning" Jada smiled and did her famous booty dance, while winking at James.
"Ooohhh, y'all nasty" laughed Mia.
"Whatever" Jada said, as she strutted into the club holding onto James.

******

Jada lay across James' chest smiling and thinking about the duet they performed at club Epiphany.
"I'm still tripping. I can't believe they gave us a standing ovation. I'm on cloud nine" Screamed Jada. James didn't hear a word Jada said, he was sound asleep. Jada sat up in bed and watching him sleep.
He looked so peaceful. She took her finger and started tracing along his goatee, down the middle of his neck, along the inner

part of his chest until she came to the lower part of his stomach. The tattooed lettering across his stomach caught her off guard. Her eyes started watering up, she put her hand to her mouth, and broke down crying. Etched in his stomach in big bold colorful letters were the words.
"Jada, you are the air I breathe when I wake up in the morning. Will you marry me?"

Chapter 15

Mia

Troy was prancing around the bedroom whistling to him-self as if he didn't have a care in the world. "Can you drop my suits off at the cleaners today on your way to work?"? He asked, still whistling

"Yes" said Mia, looking at him like he was the enemy. She had every right to look at him that way. How could he be so damn happy and gay after what he had done to her? She was just starting to feel like herself again. This last beating had really taken a toll on her body. What really had her all bent out of shape was the phone call she received a few days after visiting the clinic. The receptionist had left a message informing Mia to call the clinic regarding her blood work. When she finally got in touch with Doctor King, he informed her she had contracted a sexually transmitted disease, a STD. Mia held the phone to her ear without uttering a word. Doctor King's words kept ringing in her ear, STD...STD....When she finally realized he was still talking, she interrupted him. "What kind of STD do I have Dr. King?"

"Gonorrhea" I can call the pharmacy with a prescription for some antibiotics. You should be alright in about a week. You can follow up with your regular doctor. Would you like me to call in an extra prescription for your partner?" Asked Dr. King trying not to get too personal.

"Yes...please" Mia, still held the phone looking dazed.

"Do you have the phone number to the pharmacy to where you would like your prescription filled? Dr. Thomas, are you still there?" Asked Dr. King. The phone line was silent. Mia was sitting on the couch holding the phone pressed so hard against her ear that it was turning red. "Dr. Thomas" Said Dr. King.

"I'm still here" Said Mia looking dazed.

"Can you give me the pharmacy number?"

"Yes, I'm sorry. (313) 555-9001. " Mia was in a state of shock. It took 29 years for her to contract some type of STD, and it came from a man she stood before God to honor and obey, not some one night stand, but her husband. She felt so dirty, so un-clean. How could he disrespect their marriage by sleeping raw with some nasty ass hoe. She had taken her full dose of antibiotics for the week, but couldn't bring herself to tell Troy. She knew Troy all too well. She knew he would try and turn the tables and put the blame on her. She decided to let him find out on his own. She knew the effects of Gonorrhea would eventually surface. She had read about STD's and the different symptoms in high school. For now she was clean. She would just have to avoid from having sex with him.

****

Jada had been checking in on Mia every day to see if she needed anything. As soon as she told Jada about the STD situation, Jada hit the roof. Troy was called every doggish name in the book. Jada's only advice was; *"leave that nasty ass hoe"* She knew Jada was right, but for some reason Mia felt she had to try and save her marriage. Her thoughts drifted back to Chase. Every time she thought of him, it brought her to a happy place. She knew he was worried sick about her. They hadn't spoken to each other in over two weeks. He had left several messages at her office and on her cell phone, begging her to call and let him know she was alright. She felt dirty and cheap and she couldn't bring herself to dial his number. Every time she picked up the phone, she ended the call as soon as she punched the last digit. The love she once felt for her husband seemed to be fading away along with everything else in their marriage. She needed to talk to someone and she knew exactly who it was. It wasn't Dr. Odom, but her mother. Who better than someone who knew her inside and out? She hadn't visited her mother in weeks. This was a visit that was long overdue.

Chapter 16

Chase/Mia

"Mia you had me worried sick. Please don't ever do that again" said Chase, through the phone.

"I'm sorry Chase, it's just that I've been having some emotional problems and I didn't want to burden you with them." Mia felt a sense of comfort hearing his voice.

"You will never be a burden to me. I'm here for you Mia no matter what the circumstance. I'm only a phone call away" She held the phone thinking about the visit with her mother. She knew her mother was hurt and angry as the words spilled from her mouth describing how Troy beat her for no apparent reason. After hours of talking and crying together, it was like a pound of weights had been lifted off her shoulders. Her mother stressed that marriage and love didn't consist of a husband beating his wife. She thought her mother's point of view on her situation with Troy would be totally different from Jada's. Mia's mother shocked her with the advice she offered. She told Mia in a warm motherly tone, *to "Leave that no good son of a bitch"* Mia had never heard her mother use profanity. She sat at her mother's kitchen table silent for about sixty seconds before she burst out laughing. She fell on the floor she was laughing so hard. Before she left, she promised her mother that she would visit more often. She realized talking to her was just what she needed.

"Earth to Mia, hey are you there?" said Chase, through the phone.

"I'm sorry I was just thinking about the visit with my mother"

“A mother’s voice of wisdom is always something good to hear, especially when you’re going through difficult times. I know my mother kept me focused when I lost my wife. I don’t know what I would have done without her” said Chase.

“Yeah my mom was a comfort. I should have talked to her a long time ago. Let’s stop talking about sad things and talk about something else. Like, how have you been doing? What have you been up to”? Asked Mia hoping he would ask her out to dinner again.

I’ll be doing much better if my good friend Mia would drop whatever it is she’s doing and come by my house and have dinner with me” Said Chase, holding the phone hoping Mia would agree.
“You know what? Dinner at your place sounds good. What’s your address” Chase was silent for a moment the initial shock had not set in. He didn’t think Mia would agree to have dinner with him at his home. He had tried to convince her on several occasions but she declined every time, saying that she didn’t think it would be appropriate for her to come to his home. Now here she was without hesitation saying yes. “It’s 12672 Apple Lane in Dearborn Heights. Do you need directions”? Chase smiled through the

phone.
"I know exactly where Apple Lane is, Jada's mom lives on the next block. I should be there in about 20 minutes" Mia hung up the phone. Chase walked over to the fridge excited at the thought of Mia coming over. After observing the contents of the refrigerator, he took a deep breath and started talking to himself.
"Damn...peanut butter, jelly, butter, eggs, bacon, bob evans sausages, and some left over pizza and a frozen pot pie in the freezer" There was no sign of any kind of dinner that could be made from the contents in his refrigerator. Chase was pacing around in the kitchen trying to think of a carry out restaurant nearby. He finally put his creative juices in place and decided on making a meal from the food left in the fridge. He kept looking at the clock as he was preparing their meal.
"Five more minutes, and I should have everything in place" he said to him-self. Chase placed the food on the table, and covered each plate with a stainless steel top. He moved throughout the house lighting scented candles. He had transformed his place from a bachelor's pad to a romantic dinner setting. Everything was in place and the sound of Luther Vandross was bouncing off the walls throughout the house, *"If this world*

were mine...I would place at your feet... all that I own..you been so good to me..if this world were mineeee...." He was so memorized with the sound of Luther's voice he almost didn't hear the doorbell chimes. He stopped in front of the mirror that hung in the entrance to the hallway and took a once over glance at him-self. He had been painting all day and hoped the speed shower and the splash of Bvlgari AQVA had taken away the scent of the paint. He took a look through the peek hole and was taken aback with Mia's beauty. Chase stood at the door watching her through the peek hole. She stood at the door running her fingers through her short crop. She rung the doorbell again, and started knocking on the door with her fist. Chase stood back, opened the door and embraced Mia in his arms. They stood in his doorway holding each other. Mia didn't resist, she felt safe in Chase arms. Chase pulled back and looked at Mia. He could see her eyes watering up. "Are you alright?" He asked as he stroked her face.

"I'm okay, just glad to see you" Mia could smell the scent of Sweet pea aroma therapy.

"Wow...it smells good in here"

"Thanks, let me take your coat" Chase replied, as he helped Mia out of her coat.

His jaw almost dropped to the floor when he laid eyes on nothing but Mia's birthday suit. She stood in front of Chase butt naked, with a red pair of Michael Kors peep toe pumps. Chase stood back admiring her beauty. She walked up to him, took both his hands and wrapped them around her waist.

"Mia are you?" Before Chase could finish his sentence, Mia put her finger to his lips. She grabbed his face and pulled him to her, and started kissing and sucking on his bottom lip. Chase picked Mia up and proceeded to carry her up the circular stairs to his bedroom. He gently laid her across the bed, raised her left leg in the air and started licking the inner part of her thigh. Mia instantly started moaning, the sexual feeling she was experiencing felt so right, and soooo... good. She moved her hands between her legs and started pleasuring herself. He had never seen Mia like this. It turned Chase on. He stood up, unbuttoned his shirt and let his pants fall to the floor. He grabbed her by the ankles and pulled her down to the edge of the bed. His manhood was rock hard and swollen. You could see a clear drop of cum dripping from the tip."

"I want you inside of me" Moaned Mia, as she reached for Chase. Chase reached inside the top drawer next to the bed,

pulled out a condom and ripped the packet open with his teeth. He placed it over his swollen penis, picked Mia up off the bed, lifting her up as she wrapped her legs around his waist. He proceeded to gently place Mia's throbbing vaginal on top of his manhood. Chase eased the tip of his dick inside Mia causing her to throw her head back moaning while holding onto to him. She started a slow rhythmic motion raising herself up and down. Chase pulled out a few inches, and thrust hard, making Mia scream in ecstasy. Their moans of sexual pleasure were vibrating off the walls. They overpowered Luther's masculine tone. Mia grabbed Chase by the back of his head,
"Damn…baby, damn baby" she kept repeating as she rode with his every thrust. You could hear the sound of his balls smacking against her ass. The more she screamed, the harder he thrust his penis into her.
"Ohhh…baby" Chase moaned, as he felt the intensity of his orgasm about to explode. He gripped Mia's ass tighter, slamming her to him with every thrust.
"Mia baby, you feel so good" He fell back against the bed with Mia on top of him making sure his dick stayed inside the warmth of her juices. He rolled over on top as Mia raised her legs in the air

wrapping them around his neck as he thrust harder and harder. He grabbed her legs and held them up in the air and with every thrust she started screaming; "Yes baby, yes baby...yessss...." Her screams overpowered Chase's groans as his body stiffened up letting loose his love fluid. Mia's cum soaked his condom covered manhood, as he proceeded to pull out leaving a trial of cum along her stomach. They lay in each other's arms breathless and exhausted.

Chapter 17

Troy

It had been over a month since Troy and Taylor had been together. This last case he was working on had been taking up a lot of his time.

"Mr. Thomas you have a call on line two," said his secretary. Troy punched line two and a soft sensual voice came over the phone.

"I've missed having you inside me. Can we meet tonight?"

"Who is this?" Asked Troy smiling to himself, recognizing the sweet soft voice on the other end. He was shocked and glad at the same time. After their last encounter, he didn't' think Taylor wanted to see him again. He started rubbing between his legs getting an instant hard on while talking.

"I'm finishing up an important case can we meet tomorrow night at our usual spot around 7?"

"I'll see you tomorrow" breathed Taylor, as she smiled to herself. Taylor had her own agenda as to why she all of a sudden she wanted to see Troy. She knew he had a soft spot for her. Now all she had to do was work her charm.

Chapter 18

Mia

Mia was in heaven the last few weeks. Whenever she was around Chase, she felt relaxed and at ease. He brought out the joy in life that she had been missing for years. She knew what had to be done between her and Troy, but she didn't know how to go about dissolving their marriage. The truth was, she was scared. She knew her husband all too well, and she didn't want to bring out the demon in him. She knew once she served him with divorce papers, she would face dire consequences.

She didn't know if she could do it alone. Beep…beep….beep…. "Hello" said Mia "Hey gorgeous," said Chase. A smile spread across Mia's face as soon as she heard Chase's voice. "Hey sexy…how you doing?" Mia asked, with her Wendy Williams impersonation, still blushing like a school girl.
"I was just checking on my favorite girl" "Well…your favorite girl is good now that I hear your voice" Mia smiled as she thought about how lucky she was to have Chase back in her life. He was just what she needed. She felt good talking to him. Everything about him just felt so right. They were reminiscing about their college days.

"I remember you wouldn't even go out your dorm room without making sure your hair was in place, and don't let me forget the MAC ice lip gloss. With those sweet sexy lips" said Chase. Mia was still blushing through the phone. She missed having a man compliment her, especially someone she cared about.

Beep…beep…"Chase hold on, someone is beeping in on the other line" "Hello"

"Mia, where are you?" Troy asked. The vibe Mia was getting from his tone didn't sound good. She could tell he was on edge, or pissed off about something.

“I’m en-route to the house” said Mia

“You know you fucked up” Hollered Troy. Mia was holding the phone looking puzzled. *“What the fuck is he talking about?”* she thought to herself.

“Troy, what are you talking about?” Mia tried to ease the conversation and calm Troy down.

“The cleaners gave you the wrong damn suit. This cheap ass looking polyester suit you brought home sure in the fuck ain’t mine”

“I’m sorry Troy, I’ll stop by there on my way home” Mia’s phone was beeping again. She had completely forgotten about Chase holding on the other line.
“Troy hold on, I have to answer the other line it might be my office calling” Mia’s hands were shaking, as she punched the button on the phone. “Chase, I’m so sorry I had you on hold so long”

“Bitch this ain’t Chase” Mia dropped the phone. She sped down the ramp getting onto I-94 west trying to think of what excuse she could give Troy. Her mind was in a whirlwind of thoughts. All she could think about was *another ass whooping"* She didn't know how much more she could take.

****

Troy was pacing back and forth from the dining room, and back to the living room. You could see the veins pulsating on his bald head he was so upset. He had dialed Mia's phone over ten times and it kept going straight to voice mail. He left her a long drawn out message warning her to expect an ass whooping when she got home. He didn't appreciate the fact that she had lied to him. She was still communicating with Chase, after he had warned her to drop him as her patient. Mia had told him that she had let Chase go as a patient and had referred him to another doctor. "That bitch lied to me" Troy hollered to himself.

Chapter 19

Jada

Jada thought she was dreaming as the sound of Jaheim's voice was ringing in her ear. "Hey, how ya doing...?" Her phone was buzzing and buzzing with his ring tone. She jumped up almost falling off the couch. "Helloooo...." she mumbled, still half asleep.

"Get your ass up girl. I'm standing outside your apartment. Open the damn door" Mia said

Jada dragged herself up off the couch and made her way to the door, rubbing her eyes. “What’s up girl?” Jada asked frowning up her brow at Mia.

“I need your help, I’m in a helluva bind, and I don’t know what the fuck to do.”

“Did Troy do something to you?” Jada took Mia’s face in her hands.

“No, it’s not what you think. Troy didn’t put his hands on me yet” Said Mia

“Then what the fuck are you standing here for looking stressed the hell out?” Jada tried to make sense out of why Mia was there.

“If you would just sit down and listen I will tell you why I’m standing in your doorway looking stressed the hell out.”

“Okay, talk” said Jada looking at Mia like she was crazy. She was not the friendliest person being having her sleep broken.

“I was talking to Chase on the phone, when Troy beeped in screaming about me picking up the wrong damn suit from the cleaners, and when I tried to click back over to Chase, it was Troy on the line”

“Please tell me you didn’t call Troy by Chase’ name” asked Jada, looking worried now.

“Yes,” said Mia, as she dropped her head down” Jada pulled Mia down on the couch next to her, and held her. She knew her friend needed her now more than ever.

Jada was really scared for her, Troy was a damn monster, and she knew what he was capable of doing.
"Mia, I know you don't want to hear this, but I'm going to call Troy. I think he'll listen to me"
"I don't know Jada, I told him I was going to refer Chase to another doctor. Now that he know I lied to him, there's no telling what he's thinking"
"Well, we better come up with a good ass excuse why you were on the phone with Chase, and quick" said Jada, with concern in her eyes. Lately she had been having weird dreams about Mia that woke her up in a cold sweat. Her dreams always ended with Mia being dragged into a dark room. She hadn't told Mia about the dreams because she didn't want to worry her. Before Jada called Chase, she had a few questions she wanted to ask Mia.
"Have you been seeing Chase" Jada asked, looking at her friend.
"Yes, over the past few weeks, it's been non-stop. Almost every other day, I stop by his house on my way home, we eat, watch a movie sometimes, and then I go home. Troy is never there and he doesn't seem to care one way or the other if I'm home or not" Jada looked at Mia smiling. She was happy knowing that Mia had moved on from Troy, but she was still

concerned.
"Jada I want a divorce, but I don't know how to go about doing it without sending Troy over the edge. You know how crazy he can get. Maybe I should get a restraining order against him first"
"Mia, he's an attorney what excuse will you have for requesting a restraining order? I know, and you know, what he's capable of doing and what he has done to you in the past. But, the courts will not grant you a restraining order unless he's done some physical abuse, in which he has, or threatening your life. Are you ready to go through with this? Because you know he will eat you alive in court. Maybe we should talk to your mother, see if one of the attorneys at her law firm can advise you on how you should proceed with a divorce"
"I knew I could count on you Jada. I'm sorry I kept this from you. I didn't want you to look at me in a bad way. I know I shouldn't be seeing another man, let along sleeping in his bed when I'm married"
"Did you say sleeping in his bed?" Jada asked, with a smile on her face.
"Yes, that's what I said, and you know what? I don't feel guilty about it. I guess because I know Troy's been sleeping around with any and every woman that comes through his office. Over the years

I've received letters and text messages from women saying how they are sleeping with him. I actually followed up on one of the messages, and there was my husband exiting the Courtyard Marriott in Southfield with a female. Yet, I was the one who got beaten for checking up on him. It used to bother me in the beginning, I guess because at the time I truly loved Troy and wanted our marriage to work. But after so many years of abuse, my mind and body became numb to him and the beatings. It doesn't bother me anymore. It's as if I'm a zombie, I get up, go to work, come home, clean, cook, and go to bed. That is until now. Chase has given me a reason to get up in the morning. He's given me life, my life".

Chapter 20

Troy

The ringing of his cell phone pulled him out of his trance. "You know you got an ass swooping coming" screamed Troy, through the phone. He hadn't bothered to check his caller ID to see who was calling. "Maybe we should just post pone our date" said Taylor, sounding frantic. The image of their last encounter immediately surfaced when he hollered through the phone. She didn't want to experience anything like that again.

"Baby, I'm sorry, I thought you were someone else. You know I would never do anything to hurt you ever again" He had been drinking and the effects of the alcohol had kicked in.

"Taylor, please I need to see you" begged Troy. She was hesitant about meeting him. She had been exposed to his violent temper before and she wasn't too keen on rekindling that again.

"Troy, why don't you sleep it off and we can reschedule" The thought of him being drunk would make her plan flow smoothly, but she was still hesitant about being around him. In the back of her mind, she was scared to be alone with him. Visions of him almost choking her to death and breaking her back kept surfacing. Taylor decided to reschedule their sexual escapade.

"Troy call me tomorrow." After hanging up, she knew she had made the right decision, because ten minutes later, he called and left her a nasty message. She knew by tomorrow he would be smothering her with I'm sorry messages and sending flowers again. She knew he had demons in his past, but she didn't know the full extent of those demons. She decided to turn off her ringer and go to sleep.

Chapter 21

Jada

"He's not answering, I'll leave him a voice message" said Jada.
"It won't help" said Mia, looking tired, and worried.
"Look, I'll go home with you, I know he ain't that brave and bad to put his hands on you while I'm with you. We'll both give him the ass swooping of a lifetime he won't forget. " Jada laughed, trying to lighten up the mood. She heard the door knob turning to the apartment and knew it was James coming in. He walked in humming to himself. He was always humming some

song.
"Damn...y'all sitting in here like somebody died" He said, looking from Jada to Mia.
"James can help. He's a know how men think" Said Jada.
"Okay, what's going on" asked James, frowning up wondering where this conversation was going. Jada had already mentioned to James how Troy would beat Mia. She made him promise never to tell anyone. James didn't care for Troy after he found out he was a woman beater, especially a woman he stood before God and promised to cherish. James didn't' believe in men putting their hands on a woman. He called men like Troy cowards.
"We gotta help Mia" Said Jada. Mia was shaking her head no.
"Don't be sitting there shaking your head, you already know I ain't taking no for an answer." Said Jada. They sat down on the couch and gave James the full details of what happened, and how Mia wanted to divorce Troy. James was glad to hear she had finally come to her senses. He knew Mia didn't deserve to be treated like a punching bag. James decided that Mia could tell Troy that the only reason Chase had called her was because the doctor she referred him to was on vacation and she was covering for that doctor. It was the only reasonable solution he could come up

with. James let it be known he didn't like the fact of lying to another man, but with Troy it was the only reasonable solution. He knew Troy was crazy as hell and would probably try to kill Mia if he knew Chase was not only her patient but her lover too.

Chapter 22

Troy

There was a cold chill in the air. The room was dark as Troy sat up in bed still fully dressed and unaware of his surroundings. The liquor had taken its effect on him. He closed his eyes and started rubbing his head. He felt a migraine coming on. He looked over at the clock on the bedside stand. The red neon numbers read 3:13am. *"Where the fuck is Mia at,"* he mumbled to himself. He got up staggering almost tripping over his feet with one shoe

still on. He kicked off the other shoe while trying to maintain his balance. As he made his way down stairs, he looked over at the sofa. The image was curled up under the blanket snoring softly.
"Bitch you hung up on me and didn't bother to call back" Bam...., he punched the side of the blanket. Jada came up swinging a miniature aluminum baseball bat. The bat caught the side of his leg, and he crunched over in pain hollering. Mia came running out of the downstairs guest room.
"Troy" She hollered. He stood up limping trying to balance himself. He plopped down on the sofa while rubbing the side of his leg.
"What the fuck is Jada doing here?" he asked, scooting to the edge of the sofa. He tried to get as far away from Jada as possible. Jada stood at attention tapping the bat against her right leg. She had an "I don't give a fuck look on her face"
"I'm here to prevent you from fucking over my friend. She is not your motherfucking punching bag. You need to keep your God damn hands to yourself. And by the way, I should hit your ass again for punching me in my side you little Bitch"
"Who the fuck you calling a Bitch?" Troy hollered. As he struggled to get up from the sofa. The pain in his leg was

throbbing.

"Make a move home-boy, I'm itching to swoop your ass with this bat." said Jada, twirling the bat around as if she was about to hit a homerun.

"Stop it, both of you" Screamed Mia. Everyone in the room got quiet, Jada and Troy were staring each other down like they were ready to go to battle.

"Troy we need to talk" Said Mia

"You damn straight we need to talk" Chase sat on the edge of the sofa, clenching his fist as if he was ready to punch anything in sight.

"It wasn't what you thought when I clicked over to get the other line. Chase was my patient on a temporary basis until Doctor Ward returned back from vacation. I didn't want to tell you because I knew how you would react" said Mia, trying to explaining. She hoping Troy would believe her. Troy started rubbing his head.

"If that is what really happened, then why the fuck didn't you answer your phone when I called back?"

"To tell the truth I was scared. When you have someone who continuously beat on you for every little mishap, you stop and say to yourself; *"Maybe I should just keep this to myself because I know he's going to get angry"* Mia looked at Troy waiting for him to start hollering or cussing. He didn't utter a word. He looked over at Jada, who was rolling her eyes at him. He went limping up the stairs. Mia went upstairs behind him. She knew he wouldn't try to hit her while Jada was there.

"Mia be careful, do you want me to come with you?" Jada asked still swinging the bat looking up at Mia as she made her way up the stairs.

"No, I'll be alright, I just need to talk to Troy" When she got upstairs, Troy told her he didn't believe shit she was saying and that she better be glad Jada was there or he would've swooped her ass. "Why do you always have to use your fist to get your point across Troy. I thought we were in this together when we stood before God, family and friends confessing our love for each other. I know you don't love me anymore, because if you did, you wouldn't hurt me the way you've been doing for the last few years. I'm sorry you feel the way you do, but it's the truth, Chase was my patient on a temporary basis" Said Mia, hating the fact that she had to lie to her husband. But to avoid getting abused, she did what any woman in her situation would have done. Lie!

Chapter 23

Taylor

"Hmmmhh...I wonder who the handsome hunk sitting out in the waiting area is here to see?" Taylor said to herself as she made her way over to where he was sitting. She didn't bother to check with the receptionist to see who he was there for.
"Hi, I'm Attorney Taylor Tate," as she extended her perfectly manicured hand.
Chase stood up, smiled, shook Taylor's hand and introduced himself.
"May I ask who you are here to see Mr. Hunter?"

"Troy Thomas" Chase said, wondering who this beautiful woman was who exuded such an air of confidence.
"Are you a client?" Asked Taylor, still curious who Chase was. Chase didn't like the vibe he was getting from Taylor.
"You ask a lot of questions Mrs. Tate"
"It's Ms. Tate, M.S." said Taylor, setting the record straight that she wasn't married. And to answer your question, It's the lawyer in me, I can't help myself, I tend to ask a lot of questions. Sorry about that, if I offended you" Smiled Taylor
"No offense taken" Said Chase
"Can I get you anything to drink? Coffee, tea, water?"
"Why is she being so damn friendly" Chase thought to himself. "Do you know what time Mr. Thomas will be back in the offe?" Asked Chase.
"I can have his secretary check his schedule" Said Taylor. She made her way over to the receptionist, who was looking at Chase, then back at Taylor.
"Well Mr. Hunter, I have good news and bad news" Smiled Taylor
"Give me the good first" Said Chase
"Mr. Thomas will be in the office today, however he won't be in until after 12 o'clock, which Is three hours from now. Is there anything I can do for you?" Taylor put on her seductive smile.

“No, I’ll try and catch up with him later” Said Chase. He got up from the chair and put his jacket on and made his way over to the elevators. He could feel Taylor staring at him. When he looked back, she was standing with her hands on her hips smiling.

****

Chase wanted to confront Troy in person about Mia. He knew Mia would be upset if she knew he had come to see Troy. Chase knew he was not going to be content until he addressed all the issues that were hindering in the back of his mind. He had a few things he wanted to get off his chest, and the only way to do that was to face Troy head on.

Chapter 24

Troy

Traffic was backed up on I-75 going north. "Damn…it's 10:30 in the morning and this shit is off the hook," said Troy to himself. He kept tapping the steering wheel with his fingers, in deep thought. He decided to call his office and let his secretary know he wouldn't be in until noon. When she informed him that Chase Hunter had been in to see him, his mental state of mind turned from being professional, to down-right crazy.

"What the fuck this nigga coming to see

me for?" Troy thought, getting angrier and angrier by the minute. He had to pull himself back, He was on his way to meet a client at her home in Auburn Hills, Michigan, and he needed to focus on her case, but in the back of his head he knew Mia had hell to pay when she came home.

****

He normally didn't like meeting clients at their residence, but this client was 62 years old, and couldn't get around that well. She had been in a car accident with Pontiac police. They were chasing a suspect and slammed into the driver side of her Ford Fusion, the impact caused the door to smash into her left side causing her hip bone to be crushed. She had undergone extensive surgery to try and repair her hip. Troy knew this case was big money, and didn't have a problem going to the client.

****

He arrived back at his office around 12:45pm. As soon as he closed his office door, he immediately rung for his secretary to get in touch with Chase Hunter. She told him Chase didn't leave a number but did leave a message that he would try and catch up with him later.

Troy was prancing back and forth in his office when he heard tapping on the door.
"Come in"
"Are you busy?" asked Taylor. Troy was happy to see Taylor. He knew she would take his mind off of Chase Hunter.
"To what do I owe this visit" Smiled Troy.
"Well, you were kind of out of it the other night when I called" laughed Taylor
"I know. I apologize for that. I had a stressful day and had a few too many margarita's"
"Well, can I cash in my rain check" Asked Taylor, as she walked up to Troy and placed her hand between his legs.
"He grabbed her by her waist and pulled her to him pressing his manhood against her. She could feel his penis start to swell.
"I think we better save that for later. See you tonight same place, same time?" Troy was excited he hadn't been with Taylor in over a month.
"Ole boy can't wait to see you" smiled Troy, grabbing his crotch. Taylor puckered up her lips, blew Troy a kiss and sashayed out of his office. All thoughts of Chase had disappeared from his mind. He was deep in thought thinking about his date with Taylor.

Chapter 25

Mia

Last night's episode with Troy went better than Mia had planned. The next morning when she got up, Troy had already left the house. Jada was still stretched out on the living-room couch sleeping soundly.
"Wake up sleepy," said Mia, pulling the covers off Jada.
"Leave me alone. You know I'm a late sleeper, plus I was up late with your crazy ass husband. What time is it anyway?" asked Jada, pulling the covers back over

her head.
“I guess we both were tired, It’s almost 11:30. I don’t have to be in the office until 2 o’clock”
“Damn, must be nice being a doctor and shit, you can plan your own schedule. Your ass should still be in the bed”
“It’s not like that, my first three appointments just happened to cancel this morning. Would you please get up, I wanted to take you to Cutter’s for lunch. I’ve been craving for some steak bites all week”
“That sound good as hell. You owe me anyway for coming to your rescue. Where is that retarded ass husband of yours?” asked Jada looking around the room. Mia was standing in the doorway laughing.
“Why he gotta be retarded?” Mia was still laughing.
“Shit...you know he got more than a few screws loose. I don’t care if he do have a law degree. That nigga is crazy as hell” Jada got up stretched and started imitating Troy, while walking around the living room cussing at Mia. They both fall on the floor laughing.

****

“I’m about to jump in the shower, and get dressed” Said Mia. Jada grabbed up the blanket and pillow Mia had given her and made her way to the bathroom. While in the shower, Mia's mind was reeling with all kinds of thoughts. She still didn't know how to approach Troy with her decision to end their marriage. She knew Troy better than anyone and she truly believed he would try and kill her. As she stepped out of the shower, she could hear her cell phone ringing. She almost slipped trying to jump out and answer it. She grabbed up the phone just in time and punched the talk button. On the other line all she heard was the sound of Luther Vandross singing, *"If this world were mine". It* brought her back to the night she made love to Chase. It was playing while they made unbelievable love. She became emotional and almost hung up the phone when Chase's voice chimed in.

"Hey beautiful"

"Hey...." Mia was smiling. Every time she heard Chase's voice it seemed to relax her and bring her to a happy place.

"I called to check on you and make sure you were alright" Chase didn't mention that he had made a visit to Troy's office. He had promised Mia he wouldn't do anything stupid like go see Troy, but he had his own agenda and needed to see him face to face.

"Me and Jada are about to have lunch at Cutter's, would you like to join us?"

"Naw…you ladies go ahead and have your girl's luncheon. I have to take care of some business. I'll call you later, maybe we can have dinner at my place"

"That's sound good, I'll call you when I'm on my way, I need to take care of some business myself today"

Chase noticed the tension in her voice.

"I'm going to tell Troy I want a divorce. I don't want to put it off any longer" Chase was overwhelmed with emotion hearing Mia finally say what he had been waiting to hear.

"Mia you just don't know how happy you've made me with those words. Are you sure you want to do this alone?" Chase was concerned for her safety.

"I'll be alright, I think after last night. Jada kind of put the fear in him about putting his hands on me"

"Damn…he is a wimp if he let a woman scare his ass" They both started laughing.

"I'll call you when I'm on my way"

"Okay"

When they hung up, Chase sat back in his chair with his head down. He didn't feel comfortable with Mia confronting Troy along.

Chapter 26

Troy

"Hey sexy, you ready for tonight?" asked Troy, standing in the doorway of Taylor's office.

"Yes..., can I bring my bad girl with me she's been dying to meet you?" Taylor smiled seductively at Troy.

"Yeah, bring your bad girl, I got somebody who wants to meet her too" Troy winked at Taylor. He was looking forward to seeing her. He knew she would take his mind off of the events that had taken place the other night. Although in the back of his mind, he didn't believe Mia's story about seeing Chase and covering for the other doctor. There was history between those two and he was the arrow that wedged his way into her heart and made her leave Chase. He wasn't through with Mia by far. He planned on confronting her about that phone call whether she liked it or not. He wanted answers.

Chapter 27

Taylor

The front desk clerk greeted Taylor with her usual friendly smile.
"How may I help you Ms. Tate?" Taylor looked oddly at the front desk clerk, wanting to ask how the hell she knew her name.
"I would like a room for one night, preferably with a king-size bed" Taylor, pulled out her credit card.
"Will there be anyone else in the room?" asked the clerk, with a smirk on her face.

She already knew the history behind Taylor and Troy meeting up at the hotel. She had assisted them many times with booking their rooms. She knew exactly who Taylor was as soon as she walked through the double doors. She also wondered how Taylor could forget who she was after she had been the one to find her missing necklace. Taylor had given her a fifty dollar bill for returning it. She was kind of pissed off with the fifty dollar so called reward though. Especially since, she had taken it to a jeweler just to see what the actual value of the necklace was. When she found out it was worth $2,500 dollars, her first thought was to keep it, but after speaking with her mother, she was convinced to turn it in. The clerk was taking her time keying in Taylor's information. She could tell Taylor was getting annoyed by the way she was rolling her eyes.
"You're all set Ms. Tate. Here's your room key. Please do not hesitate to call the front desk for any assistance you may need"
"Whatever" Taylor replied, as she snatched the key card from the clerk and walked off.
"Bitch," the clerk mumbled under her breath. Taylor stopped, turned around and asked; "Did you just call me a bitch?" She looked the clerk up and down like she

wanted to jump across the desk.
"No, Ms. Tate, I didn't say anything"
Taylor turned, stuck her middle finger up in the air and kept walking toward the elevators. When she got to the room she wanted to make sure she had all her sex toys. She dumped her overnight bag on the bed. She planned on pulling out all her tricks for Troy. She walked into the bathroom and started running a bubble bath. She lit scented candles all around the room, giving it a sensual feel. She knew he would be knocking on the door any minute.

****

"Hey gorgeous" mumbled Troy, stumbling into the room.
"You've been drinking" said Taylor, now having second thoughts about their date. She needed him sober. She planned on asking him to go to his partners and consider bringing her in as a junior partner in the firm. With him being intoxicated, she knew it wouldn't go as planned.
"Me and the boys stopped by JC's bar for a drink, or two" laughed Troy, falling down on the bed. Taylor decided to go ahead with her tricks. She proceeded to undress Troy. He laid back on the bed as if he was surrendering to her. After finally getting

him fully naked, Taylor went into the bathroom and came out with a cup of hot water. She started kissing him around his neck and down below his ear. Troy grabbed her breast and started playing with her nipples.

"Damn...baby, I missed you so much," moaned Troy.

"I missed you too boo" said Taylor, as she proceeded to lip every inch of his body. She lay between his legs, reached over and brought the cup of hot water up to her mouth. She blew on it to make sure it wasn't too hot. Next she took a big gulp of water and placed her mouth over his penis. The warm sensation immediately had Troy moaning and pushing his penis further in her mouth. Taylor didn't get a chance to even start sucking, before Troy exploded. She jumped up and ran to the bathroom, spitting the water and cum into the toilet. "Damn...I hate this shit" said Taylor wiping her mouth with a rag, while walking back into the bedroom. Troy was lying across the bed butt naked and snoring.

"Ass hole" Taylor shouted. She couldn't believe he fell asleep. Normally she would wake him up, but decided to let him sleep off the liquor. She decided to take a nice warm bath surrounded by the scented candles, but before she could make her way into the bathroom, his cell phone was ringing. Taylor looked at the name flashing across the screen *"Mia"*. Taylor smiled, and hit the ignore button on his cell phone. She clicked over to the camera on his phone, took a picture of Troy butt naked and snoring, and sent it to Mia, with a message saying. *"I just sucked your husband's dick dry and knocked him the fuck out."* Taylor laid his cell phone back down on the night stand, and stood looking at Troy sleeping, while smiling to herself. She turned on the radio, and started humming along with the song playing, *"Apologize"* by the group One Republic. As she stood in front of the mirror admiring herself, she started singing along with the song, thinking about the men in her past, the abuse, and the apologies. She realized the song touched her in so many ways. She kept singing as the tears started to flow. *"You tell me that you need me, then you go and cut me down.... but wait.....You tell me that you're sorry, didn't think I'd turn around and say.....That it's too late to apologize, it's too late"* .... Although Troy apologized numerous times, there was no way she would forget. But she had her own agenda for seeing him tonight. She was on a mission and time was of the essence. She didn't care about sending the picture to Mia. She wanted payback for the crazy shit he had done from the last time they were together. What better way than to see it in print.

Chapter 28

Mia

Mia held her phone looking at the naked image of Troy. Her eyes watered up, as the tears started to escalate down her cheeks. The tears were not tears of heartache, but tears of the mental, and physical abuse she had experienced at the hands of her husband. Taking another look at the picture, Mia felt sorry for him. She knew in her heart, he would never know how to love a woman. Receiving the picture only added to her list of reasons why she no longer wanted to stay in the marriage. There was no love, joy, honesty, or hope anymore. It was time to start a new beginning, and the time was now. She looked at the clock and saw it read 8:42pm. She wanted to wait until tomorrow and talk to Troy, but after receiving the photo, it only heightened her motivation to face him head on. She went upstairs to their bedroom, and located the 357 Magnum she had purchased a month ago. She wanted some form of security when she faced him, and what better way than the hard cold steel form of a gun in her hand. She didn't plan on hurting him, she just wanted to scare him a little. She wanted to let him know that she was serious, and wanted out of their marriage. She grabbed her purse off the bed, threw the gun inside and made her way into the garage. She looked from the BMW, to the Range Rover, and decided to take the BMW. It was black on black. She knew where her first stop would be from past encounters with Troy's infidelity.

"Men never change, I know Troy is probably laying up in the same ass hotel as before" Mia thought to herself, as she pulled out of the driveway burning rubber.

Chapter 29

What's done in the dark, comes to light

Taylor had dozed off to sleep next to Troy. She could still hear the radio playing in the background and thought she was dreaming, but the cold water splashed against her face made her jump up.
"What the fuck did you do that for" screamed Taylor, as she jumped off the bed, wiping water from her face.
"Your stupid ass took my phone, took a

picture of me sleeping, and sent it to my wife," hollered Troy. He looked like a mad man on steroids. The veins in his head were pulsating. He kept pounding his fist together as if wanting to punch Taylor.

"Troy, please I can explain," cried Taylor, wishing she could turn back the clock and do everything differently. She wasn't thinking. She should have known from past experience that Troy always got up and checked his phone.

"What the fuck were you thinking?" Troy asked while walking toward Taylor with his fist clinched. Taylor didn't know what to do, or say. She was terrified. "I think it's best if I just leave" she said, walking past Troy. Bam!...Troy knocked Taylor in the back of her head as she was bending down pulling her panties up. She went falling face forward on the floor, scraping her face against the rough, cheap carpet. As she struggled to re-gain her composer, her last encounter with Troy came rushing back in her head. Her only thought was, *"This mothafucka is going to kill me"* as she was raising herself off the floor. He dropped kicked her in the back like a WWE wrestler. The impact slammed her back down on the floor. She attempted to get up again, but her body wouldn't move. She could hear Troy mumbling and talking to himself. He sounded like a

crazed madman. He kept saying the same thing over and over again.
"Bitch, see what you made me do" Taylor lay on the floor for what seemed like hours, but it had only been seconds stretching into minutes. She started praying like she never prayed before. She could hear the sound of running water coming from the bathroom. She tried to get up again but her body wouldn't move. She lay stretched out across the middle of the bedroom floor with only her panties on. She hoped and prayed that someone would hear the commotion coming from their room. Just when she was giving up hope, she could hear the sound of the hotel room door being opened.
"My prayers have been answered," Taylor thought to herself. She was too scared to scream or say anything fearing that Troy would hear her and come out of the bathroom. Unable to lift herself up, Taylor turned her head in the direction of the door. She was shocked to see Mia standing over her with a gun in her hand. Mia looked down at Taylor as if she was looking in a mirror. She knew what Taylor had experienced at the hands of Troy. Before Taylor could utter a word, Mia bent down in front of her and put her finger to her lips as if to quiet her. Taylor shook her head up and down, and looked toward

the bathroom door to let Mia know that Troy was in there. Mia got up, walked over and put her ear to the door. She listened for any type of sound or movement, but she didn't' hear anything. She knocked twice on the door, still no sound. As she grasped the doorknob, and started to turn it, the door was flung from her grasp. Troy came charging out the bathroom at Mia knocking the gun out her hand. Mia tripped over her own feet and landed on the floor next to Taylor. Troy jumped on top of her and started beating her like she was a crack head on the streets. Taylor was screaming at the top her lungs for Troy to stop. No matter how loud Taylor screamed, it didn't seem to faze Troy. He had a crazed look in his eyes, and he was on a mission. He was pounding away at Mia's face, blow after blow until Mia lay motionless on the floor.

"Oh my God, Oh my God you killed her" screamed Taylor as she dragged her body across the floor with her elbows trying to get out. Mia lay on the floor, her face splattered with blood. Troy lifted himself off the floor and plopped down on the foot of the bed. He sat there with his head down, panting trying to catch his breath. After a few minutes he lifted himself up off the bed and walked over to where the gun lay. He picked up the gun unlatched the safety, put it to the side of his right temple and let off one shot. The sound could be heard, throughout the hotel. You could hear voices shouting and footsteps running down the carpeted hallway in the direction of the room.

“Someone call 911” screamed the hotel employee, as he stepped inside the room. He saw firsthand the brutal beating Mia had just gotten, as she lay in a puddle of blood, her face looked disfigured. He looked over at Taylor struggling to get up. He went over and grabbed her up in his arms, laid her across the bed and covered her with a blanket. Taylor was moaning in pain from the blow to her back. She couldn't feel any movement from her legs. As she lay across the bed waiting for the ambulance to arrive, she closed her eyes envisioning all the warning signs that were put right in front of her face. But she chose to ignore them. Troy showed the same signs as her ex-fiancee, but Troy had deeper demons in his life. She got caught up with the notion of doing whatever it took to become a partner in the firm, even if it meant sleeping with a mad man.

Chapter 30

Chase

Chase walked out of the bathroom into the bedroom toweling off. He froze in front of the television set in a state of shock trying to grasp what the reporter had just said. He thought he was saying nooooo....in his mind, but he could hear himself screaming nooo.....out loud. He felt weak, his knees started to buckle, and his hands were shaking. He could barely keep his balance. It felt like a ton of bricks had dropped down on him. His heart was palpitating so fast it felt like it was about too explode. He lost his balance and fell back against the edge of the bed catching himself. His towel had slipped off from around his waist. He sat on the bed, butt naked rubbing the sides of his temple. *"This can't be fucking happening, it can't true, please God tell me this is a nightmare and I'll wake up any minute now"* But as Chase sat there, the report flashed across the screen again showing photos of Mia and Taylor. The reporter faced the camera and spoke into the microphone *"Two females were found beaten in a hotel room on the eastside of Detroit today. Mia Thomas, wife of suspect Troy Thomas was dead upon arrival, from blunt trauma to the head. Taylor Tate who worked with Troy Thomas at Simon and Thomas Law firm is in critical condition. Troy Thomas is being held under police surveillance at a nearby hospital for a self- inflicted gunshot wound to the head. His condition is unknown at this time"* Chase laid back on the bed as the tears started escalating down the side of his face. He was so caught up with the fact that Mia had finally made up her mind to leave Troy, he didn't follow his gut feeling. He should have gone with her. There were no words to describe the hurt and pain he was feeling right now. It felt like he was trapped in a nightmare and couldn't wake up.

Epilogue

The church was overflowing with friends and family of Mia's who came to pay their respects. It was so many people in attendance you would have thought she was a celebrity. As the Pastor approached the podium, he looked out at the people in attendance and raised his hands and began to speak. He had a powerful voice that seemed to escalate and bounce off the walls. It was as if, God was speaking through him. After the Pastor eulogized Mia, there wasn't a dry eye in the church. He spoke of her kindness, and willingness to always want to help others. The beauty she saw in everything and everyone, and how God lifted her up in his arms to bring her home and that her father was there waiting on her. Everyone was surprised and shocked when Mia's mother got up and spoke. The church was silent as she began to speak how Mia had come to her and asked her how a husband should treat his wife. She spoke of Mia's strength, courage and determination to try and make her marriage work, and how God has a reason for everything. He took away Mia's suffering, and pain and brought her to a brighter, more peaceful place. How we should leave here today knowing that Mia is at peace. The choir rose and began to sing *"Going up Yonder"*. All of a sudden Jada stood up and started walking toward the front of the church. She began clapping her hand and singing along with the choir. The Pastor handed Jada the mike. She sang with so much passion and conviction, people were shouting and jumping around in their seats. She was walking up and down the aisle with tears running down her cheeks *"Oooohhhh......I'm going up yonder......I'm going up yonder.......I'm going up yonder to be with my lord"* James got up and held Jada as she began to break down. He guided her to her seat and held her close to him. He could feel the kicking movements of their unborn daughter. Jada pressed her face into his chest trying to bury all the hurt and pain of losing her best friend and sister, Mia. With her face pressed into his chest she whispered,

"Why Lord, why?" The day had begun dark and dreary, but as the doors of the church opened, the sun was shining brightly. The pallbearers lifted the casket and proceeded down the middle aisle of the church. After the funeral, Jada, Chase and James met up at Mia's favorite restaurant reminiscing over old times. They laughed, they cried, and they promised each other that they would meet up every year on Mia's birthday to celebrate. Jada got up from her seat and said, "Let's not get caught up in life doing things that are not right, because the consequences will break you down, where even God can't save you. I pray for my sister that is finally at peace. She suffered mentally and physically at the hands of someone who stood before God and promised to protect and honor her. Tomorrow is not promised, so go home and tell your mother, father, sister, brother, aunt, uncle, niece, nephew, and cousin that they are special and you love them. Mia was my friend and the sister I never had, I can't get her back, but I can move on and do what is right in God's eyes. I made a promise to myself not to get "Caught Up". They walked away that day with a new outlook on life. You are in control of your destiny. Stand up and own it.

Caught Up

His touch once made me scream and moan

Big daddy, Big daddy, come on back home!

I was caught up with love

I was caught up with lust

But is the abuse worth it, if it hurts so much

My mind is reeling with thoughts of suicide

Your touch burns my soul deep down inside

You say that you love me

Your weapon is your hand

I made that almighty promise to stand by my man

Through thick and thin

Even through the abuse

I don't know how much more I can take

Before I have to let loose

We all love a man's touch

Is it worth it, if it's hurt so much!

Coming Soon

Hide and Seek

Gwen's first children's novel:

Bully me, Bully you!

Be sure to check out Gwen's collection of Street lit novels at www.gwencannon.net

Visit your local book store, or order online at Barnes and Noble, Amazon.com, and Borders

Everything that looks good, ain't good for you

Stuck in the Dark

Scandalous

Stuck in the Dark II

About the Author:

Gwen Cannon, a native of Detroit, Michigan, currently resides in Dearborn Heights, Michigan. She was educated in the Detroit Public School System and earned a Bachelor's degree in Business Management from Cornerstone University and an MBA in Business Administration.

In her spare time, she loves to read, cook, write poetry, play Co-ed softball—and indulge in her newest pastime, writing novels.

She was so intrigued with various novels that it inspired her to write one herself. Caught up is her fifth work of long fiction. She is happily married to her soul mate James Cannon, and they have five sons—James Jr., Corey, Jonathan, Jordan, and Jalen—and one granddaughter, Co'Mya.

Caught Up

www.ingramcontent.com/pod-product-compliance
Lightning Source LLC
Chambersburg PA
CBHW021016180626
46814CB00003B/1308

* 9 7 8 0 9 6 7 6 5 6 1 6 8 *